LAYING DOWN THE LAW

Fargo glared at Cliff, one of the "deputies" who had nearly beaten him to death less than a week before.

"Sometime in the next twenty-four hours, Cliff, I'm going to find you and put you in the hospital. And the only way you can avoid it is to pack up your things and get out of town. Tell that to your friends, too."

McGinley jumped up. "Hey! You don't run people out of town—I do!"

"Oh yeah, right," Fargo said. "I forgot. You're the high sheriff of the county."

Then, like lightning, he was on Cliff before Cliff even had time to flinch, let alone flee. Fargo grabbed him by his shirt and the seat of his pants, and fired him out the door into the dusty street. Citizens didn't like to see their law enforcement pitched out. It undermined one's faith in his local law enforcement.

Fargo turned. "See you around, McGinley," he growled. "Real soon."

Then he walked out through the open door to the street where Cliff was just starting to pick himself up, and cracked his knuckles before his hands formed into steel balls of fist.

"Like I said, Cliff, it's never too early for a fight. . . ."

THE
TRAILSMAN
#267

California
Casualties

by

Jon Sharpe

A SIGNET BOOK

SIGNET
Published by New American Library, a division of
Penguin Group (USA) Inc., 375 Hudson Street,
New York, New York 10014, U.S.A.
Penguin Books Ltd, 80 Strand,
London WC2R 0RL, England
Penguin Books Australia Ltd, 250 Camberwell Road,
Camberwell, Victoria 3124, Australia
Penguin Books Canada Ltd, 10 Alcorn Avenue,
Toronto, Ontario, Canada M4V 3B2
Penguin Books (N.Z.) Ltd, Cnr Rosedale and Airborne Roads,
Albany, Auckland 1310, New Zealand

Penguin Books Ltd, Registered Offices:
80 Strand, London WC2R 0RL, England

First published by Signet, an imprint of New American Library,
a division of Penguin Group (USA) Inc.

First Printing, January 2004
10 9 8 7 6 5 4 3 2 1

The first chapter of this book originally appeared in *Six-Gun Scholar*, the two
hundred sixty-sixth volume in this series.

The Trailsman

Beginnings . . . they bend the tree and they mark the man. Skye Fargo was born when he was eighteen. Terror was his midwife, vengeance his first cry. Killing spawned Skye Fargo, ruthless, cold-blooded murder. Out of the acrid smoke of gunpowder still hanging in the air, he rose, cried out a promise never forgotten.

The Trailsman they began to call him all across the West: searcher, scout, hunter, the man who could see where others only looked, his skills for hire but not his soul, the man who lived each day to the fullest, yet trailed each tomorrow. Skye Fargo, the Trailsman, the seeker who could take the wildness of a land and the wanting of a woman and make them his own.

California, 1861—
When one man controls a whole town,
he alone decides who lives—
and who dies.

1

Screams were not what Skye Fargo expected to hear on a gentle, moonlit night as his big Ovaro stallion worked its way along a low bluff above the Pacific Ocean.

Fargo had drifted all the way to the California coast to see an old friend who was dying, a young man in Mountain Bend. Unfortunately, the man was dead and buried before Skye could reach him.

His intention was to spend a day or two along the ocean taking in the spectacular sights and then head down to Texas to help out another friend, a marshal who was being harassed by a gang of gunnies.

But now there were screams.

On the crest of a hill to Fargo's right, he could make out the figure of a woman silhouetted against the moon-luminous night sky. She screamed as she ran down the grassy incline toward Skye. Moments later, a rider appeared, his horse moving fast. The man had a rifle and was firing round after round at the fleeing woman. Fortunately for her, she kept stumbling as she ran. She wasn't an easy target to hit.

There were those who said that the Trailsman always went looking for trouble. Not so. Trouble always seemed to find him. Here he was, loping along a bluff above the beautiful and serene Pacific, and all of a sudden he was thrust into the middle of some kind of deadly drama.

But what choice did he have?

Could he let a man kill a woman?

He turned his stallion toward her and set off at full gallop. Either the rifleman didn't see Fargo or didn't care that he was there. When he'd spent all the bullets in his rifle, he jammed it back into his scabbard and scooped up his six-shooter. He was close enough to the woman that he could easily shoot her with his handgun.

Fargo knew he had only seconds to save the woman. When she saw him, she shouted, "Help me!" and started running in his direction. She was followed closely by a hail of bullets. She wore the traditional trousers and short coat of immigrant Chinese women, the coat with a standing collar and button-up side.

When he reached her, he leaned low, grabbed her around the waist and swept her up on his lap. She must have weighed all of ninety pounds. She couldn't have been older than eighteen or nineteen, Fargo saw, a fetching Chinese woman.

Only now did the rider stop. He sat there, a silhouette in the shadowy night, still holding his handgun. It was leveled at Fargo.

"You don't figure into this, mister," the man said. "You just turn the lady over to me and you keep on riding."

"You have to help me. My name is Lala Huang. This man and some others are going to lynch my brother."

"I'm a deputy sheriff," the man said. "My name is McGinley. Now unless you want to get crosswise with the law in these parts, I'd hand her over, mister."

Sounds of the sea as it splashed on shore. Scents of clean chill air and nearby pine forests. Sight of an ocean so vast that mankind wouldn't be able to tame it in a thousand millennia.

Against this beauty and majesty, three people played out a mysterious little game that the universe at large was indifferent to.

"You really trying to lynch her brother?"

"He killed a man."

"That's not true!" Lala Huang of the sweet profile said. "My brother didn't kill anybody."

"There're witnesses, Lala Huang," McGinley said. His anger had given way to a more professional tone.

"They lie!" Lala Huang said. "You know they lie! Huang Chow wasn't even there. He was with me."

McGinley came close enough for Fargo to get his first good look at the deputy. Chunky in flannel shirt and jeans, wearing a vest on which hung a silver star, McGinley said, "Set her down, mister. And there won't be any trouble."

"No!" Lala Huang said, grasping Fargo's arm. "You must come with me and stop the lynching. We don't have long!"

"Did her brother have a fair trial?" Fargo asked McGinley.

"Wasn't time," McGinley said. "He killed a nice old man this afternoon. The town wants him dead. There wasn't time for a trial."

Just then, the sound of a shotgun cracked across the sky.

"One thing I know how to do is count," Fargo said. "And I'd be willing to bet you a good amount of money that you're out of bullets in that six-gun of yours. So I'll tell you what. I've got five shots left in my Colt here. But I'll promise not to shoot you if you take me to where this lynching party is."

Another roar of a shotgun.

Fargo said, "What's going on?"

"I wish I knew." McGinley sounded worried. "Let's head over that way."

Lala Huang half-sobbed. "I hope he isn't dead already."

"Let's get going," Fargo said.

Deep in a small valley, three men stood holding torches in front of a young Chinese man who sat a horse while a noose was dropped over his head and cinched about his neck. He was dressed much like his sister and his hair was braided in the traditional Chinaman's queue, or pigtail.

The flames of the torches cast everybody into a lurid, ugly light that lent the faces of the lynchers a sinister cast, eyes sunk deep and angry, beard stubble looking greasy and filthy, mouths drooling from the rotgut whiskey they'd been drinking all night.

The exception to this was a fourth man. Tall, middle-aged, arrogantly handsome, he wore a suit of imported British tweed, used a wolfshead cane to walk with, and issued orders that not even Duncan, the sheriff, argued with. This was the richest man in the valley, Del Manning.

Manning strode over to the tree and pointed his cane at the man in the tree working the noose. "I want this clean and fast."

"Yessir, Mr. Manning." He was another of Duncan's deputies. "Yes, sir." His voice trembled when he spoke. Mere mortals rarely got a chance to work directly with Del Manning.

Then Manning addressed the young man with the noose around his neck. "Huang Chow, you really disappointed me."

"I didn't shoot him, Mr. Manning. I swear I didn't."

"He caught you stealing something from my study and you shot and killed him."

"I didn't, I didn't." Huang Chow had been pleading his innocence all day long. But he was weary now. And you could hear that in his voice. Even when your life is at stake, the strength to keep begging fades after several hours. He sounded terrified but he also sounded worn out.

Manning wasn't finished. He spoke in a grand voice, an actor addressing an audience, one hand dramatically clutching the lapel of his tweed jacket, his weight leaning on his fancy cane.

"I took you into my house, Huang Chow. Took you in and helped educate you and fed you and paid you.

And the same with your young sister. I tried to be a real father to you and then you killed Li Ping."

At any other time, Duncan and his deputies would have been muttering curses and threats. This was a lynching, after all, and there were certain things that a lynch mob should do to honor the moment. Cursing and threatening were a mandatory part of this particular ceremony. So was spitting on the prisoner. Hell, what kind of lynching was it when you didn't spit on the prisoner?

But they were too afraid of Del Manning's quirky and formidable temper to say anything. Sheriff Duncan had told them to be quiet and let Manning run the show.

"But you heard what I told our hangman up there, Huang Chow. Even given how disappointed I am in you, I told him to make this execution fast and clean. I don't want you to suffer any more than you have to."

"But Mr. Manning, please—I—"

Manning took his hand from his lapel and held it up in a way that demanded silence of Huang Chow. "You've had your say and now I had mine. Let's get on with it. I don't like this any better than you do, Huang Chow. I want to get it over with and forget about it."

The hangman, sitting on the heavy hardwood branch the rope was tied around, said, "You just say the word, Mr. Manning."

"If you'd been listening carefully, you fool, you would have *already* heard me say the word. Now hang him and let's get it over with."

And that was when the bullets started flying over the heads of the three lawmen and Del Manning, all of the men around the hanging tree responding the same way, by throwing themselves to the ground and grasping for their own weapons.

Fargo didn't want to kill anybody but he did want to stop the lynching, even one with a sheriff standing by. What the hell kind of town was this where a sheriff didn't honor a man's right to a fair trial but instead took him out to a hanging tree in the dead of night?

As he stormed toward the small group of men, he glimpsed the bloody carcass of a wolf, which might explain the shotgun blasts. There probably hadn't been any reason to kill the wolf but most people hated and dreaded the misunderstood animals so much that they killed them on sight.

He put a bullet into the tree, knocking the hangman off his branch. The man hit the ground with a startled cry.

Lala Huang pitched herself from Fargo's stallion even before the animal stopped completely. She ran to her brother.

One of the deputies started to aim at Fargo but the Trailsman blasted the gun out of the man's hand. Then he swung around and did the same thing to a second deputy.

Duncan was too seasoned a lawman to go up against what he'd just seen. He picked himself up, dusted himself off and said, "You made a bad mistake, mister."

"The name's Fargo."

"A bad mistake, Fargo. A real bad one. You interrupted a solemn ceremony of law."

Fargo laughed. "Sure I did. Dead of night. A man who hasn't had a trial. Out in the middle of nowhere. Sounds real legal to me."

"Well, I'm the sheriff and maybe this is how we conduct the law around here, you ever think of that?" Duncan said.

And then Fargo was surprised to see a tall and somewhat dandified man step from the shadows behind the tree and walk into a patch of moonlight. He was a little too dandy for Fargo's tastes but he did have a strong presence. He also carried a fancy long-barreled gun that looked to be specially made. Fargo hadn't known the man was here till now. The man could easily have shot Fargo when he rode into the situation at hand. Fargo wondered why he hadn't. It was obvious that the sheriff would have been glad to see Fargo killed.

Fargo used his gun. He signaled for the man to drop off his horse and stand with the others. "Get their guns, Lala Huang."

She complied with clear delight. Two of the deputies cursed her as she relieved them of their weapons.

"You," Fargo said to the hangman, "get that rope off his neck."

"You ain't the sheriff."

"That's right. But I'm the man who's going to shoot you if you don't."

"Do what he says, Biff." The sheriff looked awful unhappy about saying it. His face was seamed with age in the flickering light of the torches that had been jammed into the ground.

Biff walked over to Huang Chow and proceeded to extricate the man from his ropes. First he took out a knife and sawed through the rope on Huang Chow's wrists. Then he had Huang Chow lean over and removed the rope from around his neck. Huang Chow sat motionless for a spell, a slender man in his midtwenties who obviously couldn't quite believe that his life had been spared. At least for the moment.

He eased down from his horse, touching his neck where the rope had been, and then went over to stand next to Lala Huang and Fargo. Lala Huang held four guns in her arms.

"You're letting a guilty man go free," Duncan said.

"I'm not letting anybody go free," Fargo said.

"What's that supposed to mean?"

"It means, Sheriff, that I'm taking him back to your jail. And then I'm going to make sure he gets a trial. A fair one."

Huang Chow said, "No! No! You might as well have let me hang right here. There won't be any fair trial for me. They have witnesses who have lied against me. It'll be the same thing. All over again. I'll hang for sure."

"No," Lala Huang said, "listen to me, brother.

7

Fargo is right. The only way you can help yourself is to go back and face your accusers. Let there be a trial."

"I'll stick around," Fargo said. "I'll make sure the sheriff here cooperates."

"You don't know these men. They're bad men. They wear badges to hide behind. They cheat and steal and kill all the time."

"Shut up, Huang Chow," Manning said. "You know better than that. We have a fine sheriff's department. It's not their fault you killed a good man." Manning had moved up to stand near Huang Chow. He kept his gun in plain sight, making it clear to Fargo that he had no plans to fire. If he did, he obviously knew that Fargo would kill him long before he was able to raise his weapon.

"Get on your horses and ride back to town," Fargo said. "We'll bring your guns in with us."

"I'll make you a deal," Duncan said. "You actually bring this man in and I won't charge you with anything. And I'll see that he gets the kind of trial you want. But if you make me come after you—you'll be damned sorry. And I promise you that."

"You'll get him, all right," Fargo said. "And then we can start in on the trial."

That was when it happened, Huang Chow reaching over to the pile of pistols in his sister's arms and grabbing one of them. "No, I won't go back. I won't!"

"Don't make it any worse for yourself, brother. Please listen to Fargo. Do as he says!"

Sheriff Duncan started stalking toward Huang Chow, apparently under the impression that the man wouldn't actually shoot him.

"Stay back!" Huang Chow shouted, easing himself back toward a horse that he could escape on. By now, he'd reached one of the deputies' ground-tied animals. He kept his gun aimed steady at Duncan's chest. "I'm not going to warn you again!"

"I'm not afraid of you, Huang Chow," Duncan said. "I'm not afraid of you at all."

Then everything lapsed into turmoil. A gunshot. A scream from Duncan. The lawman clutching his chest. His deputies lurching toward him to help. Huang Chow throwing himself up on the horse. Fargo moving toward him, ready to wound Huang Chow in the arm and leg to make a getaway unlikely. But just as he was about to fire, Lala Huang grabbed Fargo's gun arm and pushed it off target. His two shots went wild, giving Huang Chow time to make his escape.

When Fargo turned around, Manning was down on his haunches taking the lawman's pulse. When he stood up, his knees cracking, he said, "I'm posting a five-thousand-dollars reward for Huang Chow—dead or alive. Preferably dead."

He didn't need to say that the sheriff had been murdered. Everybody understood that already.

2

Five minutes later, Fargo and Manning traveled a stretch of grassy plain filled with enough ruts and holes to slow their progress. This was dangerous terrain for horses.

This was the direction in which Huang Chow had set off. The two men, limned by moonlight, said nothing to each other. There was nothing *to* say. They both knew what had to be done. Huang Chow had killed a lawman in cold blood. The lawman might have been corrupt but it didn't matter. Huang Chow had to pay for his crime. There wouldn't be much mercy shown when they finally caught up with him. They'd offer him one chance to throw down his gun and hand himself over without any hassle. If he didn't, he'd be killed on the spot. Fargo wasn't bloodthirsty but there were times when there was no other choice.

Just before they reached a stand of jack pines, Fargo heard the cries of a horse in great pain. He signaled for Manning to follow him. Fargo cut west, searching for the source of the sound.

He didn't have to look for long. The horse lay on its side in some buffalo grass.

Fargo dismounted and hurried to it. Even from here, he could see the white jut of bone. In stumbling and falling, the horse had cracked its foreleg.

Fargo knelt next to the grieving animal, stroking its crest, muttering words meant to soothe, the way a prayer would.

"Let's get going," Manning said. "He's in those woods."

"I need a few more minutes here."

"Well, the hell with you. Shoot the sonofabitch and get it over with. It's just a horse."

Shooting you would be a lot more pleasurable, Fargo thought as Manning spoke his sneering words. Fargo turned back to the animal, continuing to speak to it and stroke its crest. If there was any other option, Fargo wouldn't shoot it. But they were in the middle of open territory, nothing around.

He took his six-shooter. He'd had to put more than one horse down in his day. The worst of it was when the first shot didn't do the job. The poor animal was put through more misery and terror than it deserved. He had his share of nightmares about it over the years, the image of the horse's eyes and the memory of the noises it had made burned into his unconscious mind.

"I'm sorry, son," Fargo said.

He put his Colt against the eyepit and fired upward twice. The top of the head flew off like a bloody cap. The horse spasmed violently and had time for just a single lonesome horrified cry. A spray of its blood misted across Fargo's face. He didn't give a damn. In fact, it was an honor to carry some of the animal's blood. He had an irrational thought about killing Manning. All the Mannings in the world who didn't understand animals and their true kinship with human beings.

Manning waited for him at the edge of the tree line, having apparently decided that it would be better to have a partner than go inside the deep darkness alone.

They didn't speak. Fargo led the way. Broken patterns of moonlight in the rough-barked trees. The almost suffocating sweetness of pine. The narrow trail sleek with pine needles. And somewhere in the distance to the west the scent and sound of the ocean.

Huang Chow had picked a good place to hide, especially if he was good at climbing trees. That was the trouble with hunting somebody in a woods this dense.

He could be hiding behind a tree—or up one. He could, if he wanted to, open fire at will and you'd never even glimpse him before he'd pumped two or three shots into you. And there wasn't much doubt that Huang Chow was the kind who'd kill you in cold blood. He'd shown the sheriff no mercy, that was for sure.

A rustling in heavy undergrowth to their right.

Both men stopped. The only sound for a long empty second was the coarse noise of their breathing. They'd been moving fast and were winded. Fargo figured the only way they were going to find Huang Chow was to let him get a shot or two at them and just hope that he missed. By walking fast they provided him with less of a target.

But something was going on in the undergrowth.

Both men crouched down, guns pointed in the direction of the loud rustling noise.

Each second seemed to take hours to pass. And it took several seconds before they finally learned what had caused the noise.

A mother raccoon with six tiny babies marched proudly from the undergrowth, turned left and proceeded to walk in the opposite direction down the trail. Fargo smiled. He liked raccoons, identified with their reputations as somewhat dangerous outcasts. A lot of people saw him that way.

Their trek continued. They didn't speak. Manning stopped once to empty his bladder. The noise he made slashed through the silence. By the time he finished, Fargo was far ahead on the trail.

Fargo saw the clearing. The woods weren't as deep as he'd expected. He stood at the edge of the clearing and saw the cabin. Smoke came from a crude tin chimney. Dirty lantern light bloomed in the half-open doorway. The only sound was the squeaky sleeping noises made by a mule resting in long grass next to the cabin.

A gunshot cracked on the still air. Inside the cabin, a shout.

The man who burst out of the door bore no resemblance to Huang Chow. He was tall, bald, white, and clad only in a red union suit and a pair of lace-up miner's boots.

He obviously had no idea where he was running, he was just running, his knees coming up fast and hard, his skinny arms awkward sticks that didn't seem to know what they were doing with themselves. In most situations, Fargo would have laughed at the crazy bastard. But now was neither the time nor the place.

"Over here!" Fargo shouted.

The man stopped in his tracks, cocked his head, and peered ahead as if he were trying to see what lay at the end of a long, dark cave.

Maybe his eyes hadn't adjusted to the night yet. Maybe he wasn't wearing his eyeglasses. Maybe he was blind.

"Over here, you stupid sonofabitch!" Manning snapped. Even now, he was arrogant. It was second nature.

The old man used their voices as a homing signal. He started lifting his knees high again and hightailed it right to where the two men stood at the edge of the clearing. Then he stumbled. The ground here was as rutted and hole-filled as that on the other side of the woods.

"Got a Chinee in there with a gun!" the old man said. "Jumped him about a minute ago and the gun went off and I beat it out the door! Surprised he didn't shoot me in the back! You know how them Chinee are!"

"You two stay here," Fargo said. "I'll go in and get him."

"Somebody make you the boss, did they?" Manning said.

The old man giggled. "You two fellas don't get along no better'n me and that Chinee."

Fargo figured that the old man was having a grand old time. Probably got lonely this far from town and here he was in the center of some pretty angry goings-on. He'd be talking about this to his mule for years.

Fargo said, "His sister got me into this. Maybe he trusts me a little more than he does you."

"Well, since it's my town and my sheriff who got killed, I think it's my right to bring him in."

"C'mon," Fargo said, "we'll both go."

Fargo had the idea that maybe Huang Chow could be brought in peacefully. You had to give him that one-time chance, anyway. He wasn't sure Manning saw it that way.

The men set off, leaving the old man behind.

"I want to give him a chance to give himself up."

"And that's what he'll get," Manning snapped. "A chance. One chance."

They stopped at the midpoint between forest edge and cabin, out of range for the kind of weapon Huang Chow had.

Fargo cupped his hands over his mouth and said, "Huang Chow, you listen to this and listen real careful. You've got thirty seconds to come out that door with your hands up. The first thing you do is throw your gun out the door. And then you follow it right out. If you don't, we'll kill you. That's the way it's going to be. And it's thirty seconds starting right now."

"I didn't shoot him," Huang Chow said.

"Sounds like your speech did a lot of good, Fargo."

Fargo didn't want to face Lala Huang with word that her brother was dead. But what choice did he have? Fargo wasn't sure about the first murder, whether Huang Chow had committed that or not. But he'd seen Huang Chow commit the second one. About that there could be no doubt.

The gun glinted in the moonlight as it arced through the air and landed on the ground. And moments later, Huang Chow scraped the cabin door wide and began walking free of the shantylike structure.

His hands were above his head. He walked with a nervous vitality. He covered half the distance between them in just a few seconds.

Fargo didn't know if Huang Chow would live to hang but at least he'd live long enough to have jail visits with his sister and maybe help her cope with the notion of his execution—the same kind of execution he'd visited on the sheriff.

And then he stumbled.

His arms windmilled in a frantic effort to keep him upright. His voice cracked with a cry. His body traveled quickly toward the ground.

But before Huang Chow was able to reach the ground, Manning put three shots in him.

Fargo reacted instinctively, reaching over and seizing Manning's gun wrist. He didn't stop there. He drove a steel fist into Manning's gut so hard that the man not only doubled over but also began choking and then puking.

Fargo ran to Huang Chow, forgetting how rutted the land was here.

Dropping to one knee, a strange thought came to him. Not long ago he'd knelt next to a horse who was about to die. The way blood spasmed from Huang Chow's mouth, it was obvious that Huang Chow was near death, too.

Fargo slid his arm under the man's head to keep him from choking on the blood. But even with his head held off the ground, Huang Chow couldn't speak. His glazed eyes said that he was only minutes if not seconds away from the final darkness. They seemed to see not Fargo but beyond him.

Fargo thought of Lala Huang. Of having to tell her about her brother. But she'd seen how cold-blooded he'd been with the sheriff. Maybe that would help her understand that her brother really was a killer who was a reckless and dangerous man.

The longest sigh Fargo had ever heard came from Huang Chow. And then came a shudder that was like a tremor deep inside the body, starting at the shoulders and then jumping to the elbows and then the knees and then the feet and then there were just the sounds of night, wind in pines, sea on shore.

"You're going to be damned sorry for this, you bastard," a voice said behind him.

He'd had the pleasure of forgetting about Manning for a few seconds. He eased Huang Chow's head down to the ground and said, "He didn't have a gun." He stood up.

"I didn't know that." Manning's face was a turmoil of pain from his broken wrist.

"The hell you didn't. You saw him throw his gun out."

"He would've hanged, anyway."

"Maybe so. But that didn't give you any right to kill him."

Manning gripped his wrist, grimaced. "I want you out of town by dawn. If you're not, you're going to be in a lot of trouble."

Fargo didn't say anything. He leaned down and spent a long moment struggling to get purchase on the corpse. He got enough of a grip to lay Huang Chow across his shoulder. Then he set off, walking past Manning without a word.

The three deputies drew pieces of hay to see which of them had to go tell Mrs. Duncan that her husband had been murdered. McGinley drew the shortest one.

He walked over to where Lala Huang sat tensely on a small boulder near the tree where they'd been going to hang her brother. She whispered words in Chinese that McGinley assumed formed a prayer.

"Should make you go and tell the missus," he said. "Your damned brother was the one who killed him."

"He was afraid. He knew that you would hang him, even though he was innocent." In the moonlight, her lovely small face glittered with tears.

"Well, he sure as hell isn't innocent now. You seen him kill Duncan same as I did."

What could she say? She was so ashamed of what Huang Chow had done. And yet she loved him, too. Despite what he'd done, she loved him as much as ever.

McGinley said, "You get yourself a lawyer and bring him over to the jail tomorrow. Your brother's gonna need all the help he can get. I might even ask the judge if I can move him to another county. People in town just might storm the jail."

"Oh, no," she said. "Please don't say that."

"Dunc had his enemies. But mostly he had friends. Folks liked him."

She looked up when she heard the horses. They were near and coming closer at a good pace. She lifted herself up from the boulder, swept off her bottom with a slender hand, and walked toward the edge of the small area where the deputies' horses stood.

In the silver light from the sky, she saw Fargo and Manning. They rode side by side but with many feet between them, as if they didn't want to talk to each other.

She didn't see the body slung across the back of Fargo's horse until they came much closer. And that was when she began screaming.

3

When Fargo got her back to the edge of town, to the tiny one-room cabin where she lived alone, he took the pint of whiskey he'd originally purchased to share with his friend in Mountain Bend and poured her half a glass full. She resisted but he insisted. Her first sips were tentative and she made kid-faces to show how the whiskey burned her throat and incited a riot in her stomach. She continued making faces through occasional jolts of tears and torn sobs.

"He didn't kill Li Ping," she said several times. "They were best friends. My brother and Li Ping even took a trip together about a month ago. You don't kill a friend like that."

Fargo sat in a chair and watched her slowly give in to sleep. She didn't want sleep, said she felt guilty about sleeping when her brother lay dead in the mortician's back room, said she would never sleep again. She said this angrily, like it was an oath, only her body was too weak to raise a hand, and soon enough she was overwhelmed by a deep slumber that would not be denied.

Fargo went on into town. He took his stallion to the livery and then strode over to the sheriff's office. He got there just in time to see McGinley sworn in by a sleepy ancient judge who'd forgotten to bring his store-bought teeth along for the occasion and who wore his nightshirt beneath a duster that looked like it hadn't been worn in years.

The eyes on him were cold when he came through the door. The eyes shifted from him to Manning. It was Manning who ran the town. Manning who made the decisions. Manning whose judgment was required. But at this point he was apparently passive on the subject of Fargo. He didn't send out any silent message. Just concentrated on the little ceremony, though at one point his gaze went to the various WANTED posters on the wall. There were three posters for a recent robbery of a huge gold shipment.

$5000 FOR ANY INFORMATION LEADING TO THE CAPTURE OF THE MEN RESPONSIBLE FOR THE MURDER OF A WAGON GUARD AND THE ROBBERY OF MORE THAN A QUARTER MILLION DOLLARS IN GOLD.

Fargo had been hearing about this since he'd reached California. One of the biggest gold robberies in history, with a dead guard on top of it.

When Fargo returned his attention to the ceremony, he had to swallow down a laugh. You could barely understand what the judge was saying. He needed his teeth. The other deputies didn't exactly complement the moment, either. They kept yawning. One of them farted and looked around guiltily to see if anybody had noticed. Quite a solemn occasion here.

The judge finished his mostly incomprehensible reading of the swearing-in and then pinned the sheriff's badge on McGinley's leather vest, sticking him in the process. McGinley jerked violently as the pin on back of the badge stabbed him. The deputies glanced at each other and smiled.

As the ceremony came to a close, the front door of the sheriff's office opened and a nervous, round little man in a black suit and soiled white shirt came in. Fargo quickly saw that the discoloration on the shirt was blood.

"I worked up the body," the man said to Manning. "Is the county going to pick up my expenses?"

"We always do, don't we, George?" Manning said.

"Mortuary's got to make a profit like any other kind of business," the man said.

"I understand. Now quit whining and get the hell out of here." Manning's contempt for the little man was easy to see.

"You say Huang Chow shot him?" the undertaker said.

"Yes."

"With his own gun?"

"As I recall, his sister had all the deputies' guns. He grabbed one of them to kill the sheriff."

"Hmm," the undertaker said. "Curious." He nodded to McGinley. "Congratulations on making sheriff, son. You'll do a good job."

"Thanks, Mr. Martin. I appreciate the kind words."

"I didn't like how you gussied up Mrs. McCollum last week," the old judge snapped. "Made her look like a whore. Everybody at the Methodist church where I go said that and I agree with them."

It was clear from George Martin's patronizing smile that he considered the old judge a crank. "Well, next time I'll try to do better, Your Honor."

"And just what can I do for you, Fargo?" Manning said, the harsh tone of his voice making everybody turn toward him, Fargo included.

"Lala Huang is home now and sleeping. I hope you'll treat her right and answer any questions she has. She's a good woman and she loved her brother."

"He was a killer."

"Yes, he was. I saw him with my own eyes. But that doesn't mean she didn't love him. Try to keep an eye on her. She's going to have some bad times in the next couple of months."

"Lala Huang isn't your business and neither is this town," Manning said. "And what I said about you being gone still goes."

"I'm going to sleep for a few hours and then go."

"Far away," Manning said, "and fast."

Fargo nodded.

Nobody said good-bye as Fargo made a silent exit.

The only sound was that of his boot steps on the wooden floor. Steps that led across the threshold out onto the board sidewalk. Steps that started across the street and stopped abruptly.

George Martin's question about the gun Huang Chow used to kill Sheriff Duncan kept coming back to him. Why was the gun so important? He was dead and that was all that mattered. But was it?

Behind him, the front door of the sheriff's office opened. A lash of lantern light fell across Fargo's back. He decided to wait for the undertaker. Fargo hated going to bed when an important question was dangling unanswered.

George Martin did not speak to Fargo, but walked right on past, headed for the mortuary down at the edge of town. The front door of the office closed and Fargo was cast into the sleepy darkness.

He walked fast and caught up with Martin. "I need to ask you a question."

"Better not, son. Manning don't like you. And if Manning don't like you and he sees us talking, he'll blame me for it. Last time I did something he didn't like, he threatened to open up his own mortuary and run me right out of business. How about them apples?"

"All I want to know is why you said there was something curious about the gun that killed the sheriff."

"I can't talk to you, mister. Good night."

And with that, he strode off in the direction of his business. He probably slept upstairs with the corpses downstairs. That was the usual layout. Fargo wasn't sure he could do that. While he didn't believe in ghosts and goblins, the idea of sharing your home with the dead . . . well, there had to be better ways to live.

He had no inkling that anything was wrong as he slid the key into the lock of his hotel room door five minutes later. He was too preoccupied with what the undertaker had found "curious." What was so damned curious about a gun, anyway?

He pushed the door inward and entered his room. Immediately he caught the sweet heady scent of perfume.

He started to reach for his Colt when a female voice said, "Don't tell me you're afraid of a woman, Mr. Fargo? That certainly isn't your reputation."

"Who the hell are you?"

"You wouldn't recognize the name even if I gave it to you. Now why don't you get those clothes off and slide into bed next to me? I think we could have some fun together."

"Sure we could," Fargo said. "Especially if you have a knife. You could open me up in the dark and I wouldn't even know it till it was too late."

"Oh, well, Mr. Fargo, if you insist."

A lucifer was scratched into stunning flame and applied to the wick of a kerosene lamp whose chimney sat next to the lamp base. She turned the flame up and replaced the chimney. What took form in the soft light was a voluptuous blonde with one of those slightly heavy faces that seem to be all about sex and little else. The sumptuous breasts appearing above the line of covers confirmed that impression. They were not only large but ended in pink nipples that made Fargo—despite his weariness and suspicion of this whole set-up—feel a stirring from within. The lady's blue eyes held intelligence and humor. She was going to be damned hard to resist, Fargo knew, responding to the tight and growing signals in his groin. He tried not to look at the elegant column of her neck, at the small shapely ears, at the moist mouth that moved with such erotic ease.

She threw the covers back. She was completely naked. And she was spectacular, from the narrow but very female hips, to the daring thatch of pure blond pubic hair, to the trim ankles and the small, well-turned feet.

"Why don't you come over here and at least sit down on the bed? Maybe you could build us a couple of cigarettes. My husband doesn't like it when I smoke. But then, I really don't give a damn what my husband likes or doesn't like, do I, Mr. Fargo?"

Coy, self-assured, and relentlessly sexy. What the hell was a clean-living man supposed to do? He was supposed to do just what Fargo did, go over and sit down on the bed and build them a couple of smokes and pretend he wasn't taking a gander at those breasts of hers every chance he got.

"You have a name?" Fargo said.

"You may not want to hear it. Not my last name, anyway. My first name is Faye."

"Why wouldn't I want to hear your last name?"

"I'm told my husband doesn't like you very much."

Fargo stared at her. He was beginning to gather some idea of what was going on. The night got crazier—and perhaps deadlier—as each moment ticked by. "He send you up here?"

"Hardly."

"So you came up on your own?"

She smiled. "Surprised?"

"Suspicious more than surprised."

She laughed. She had a good, warm, womanly laugh. "I suppose I'd be suspicious, too."

"So what do you want from me, Mrs. Manning?"

"Why look at that," she said, as if she was surveying a prime stud horse. "He's not only handsome, he's smart, too. Maybe even a mind reader." When she laughed her storm of blond hair spilled back against the white pillow. She had the kind of tight, white flesh and radiant, reckless eyes that promised a sultan's woman's knowledge of carnal skills. "My husband is good at many things. Unfortunately, making love isn't one of them. So from time to time I go on what I like to call 'excursions.'"

"In the middle of the night?"

"He wasn't home. He was going to hang our servant, Huang Chow. When he gets involved in law business, he rarely makes it home before dawn." She took his hand. "I saw you in Mountain Bend the other day, Mr. Fargo, and knew that I had to have you. That's all this is about. Pure lust. I don't know what my husband has against you—or you have against him—but I do know that I need some excitement in my life. My husband didn't marry me, he procured me, the way you would a beautiful statue you like to show visitors when they come to call. I thought an easy life like that would be exotic, but it's not, it's dull. Very dull." She took his hand and placed it over the sumptuous flesh of her right breast, the nipple peeking up through his fingers. "Take my dull away for me, Mr. Fargo. For a little while, at least."

She held her arms out to him. A cosmic force seemed to steer him in her direction, one threatening to burst his britches. He liked her perfume and the way her full breasts swayed slightly when she moved.

He knelt on one knee on the edge of the bed while she expertly followed that same cosmic force into his pants. She freed him quickly and used his manhood to tug him closer to her. She licked her lips, preparing to explore him with her tongue. In moments, she had him on his back and was stripping him down so that she could move herself up his body, plunging her tongue into his mouth while she began to rub her warm, furry sex against his growing shaft.

He knew he was in for some kind of ride, one he needed badly, as it had been a while. He consumed her full buttocks with his hands as she guided him into her. She was already very wet. She bent over him, giving him the opportunity to play her like an instrument with his tongue to her nipples. A woman's breasts were naturally sensitive; hers were on a hair trigger, as the slightest touch charged her to writhe in pleasure. Now that he was inside her, she began to thrash and wrench and spasm almost insanely, like a sexual locomotive that was out of control.

He matched her lunge for lunge, thrill for thrill. In their climax they made enough noise to wake the entire west coast, and neither one of them gave a damn, either.

4

The knock came early, too early.

The Trailsman could usually get by with four hours of sleep. He was young enough and vital enough to function like this for a night or two. The problem was he hadn't been sleeping well lately and was in bad need of a full six hours. When Faye left shortly after their love making, Fargo thought he had a chance but he wasn't to get it. Not in this town, anyway.

His first response to the knock was to consider grabbing the Colt he kept under his pillow and putting several bullets dead center through the door. He was bound to hit somebody that way.

His second response was more civilized. He'd lie in bed and shout obscenities at the stupid bastard, obscenities so devout and lurid that the man's ears would immediately be consumed in flames.

His third response, given the timidity of the knock, was to consider all the things that had happened in the past twelve hours. Given all the craziness, he'd probably better answer the door and find out who it was.

The trouble was, once he got his pants on and the door open, he had no idea who it was, just some small man with a twitchy little brush of a mustache and a walleye on the right side of his face.

The man whispered, straightening the lapels of his dusty black suit, "D. F. Tomlinson, Mr. Fargo." He then opened his closed palm. A bullet lay there. An elongated and oddly shaped bullet. Fargo had never seen its likes before.

"C'mon in," Fargo said, rubbing his hand on his mussed hair.

"I know it's a little early."

"A little early? Hell, it's still night."

"I know. But I didn't want anybody to see me. I could get myself killed for this."

"Then how come you're doing it?"

"Because Manning hated my younger brother. He planted some bank loot in my brother's house and got him sent to prison for eight years. He died there; beaten to death in the yard by another inmate twice his size."

"Sorry to hear that." Fargo put his hand out. "Let's see that bullet again."

As Fargo looked over the bullet more closely, D. F. Tomlinson paced, which wasn't easy in a room this small. "Who are you exactly, Mr. Tomlinson?"

"I work for the mortician. I help the doc with the autopsies, too."

The bullet took on profound significance once Tomlinson told Fargo where he worked and what he did. He had a suspicion what Tomlinson was going to tell him.

"That came from Duncan."

"Deputy McGinley'll say that's impossible. He'll tell you that Huang Chow grabbed one of the guns belonging to the deputies and shot Duncan with that."

"Then he'll either be wrong or lying."

"I can see why you're scared," Fargo said. "This bullet probably came from Manning's gun."

"That's what I thought. Nobody else around these parts has got a special-made gun like that. Nobody else could afford it."

"I'd like to keep this."

"Oh, no, Mr. Fargo, I can't let you do that. My boss usually gets to the mortuary about dawn. I have to have this bullet back there by then. But I wanted you to see it."

"Well, I appreciate that."

"I want to see that whole crew brought down, Mr. Fargo. From Manning straight down through the town council and the sheriff's office. We need to start from scratch in this town. All new officials. If you can prove that Manning killed Duncan, you can shake up this whole town. And lots of people will be grateful, believe me."

Fargo thought back to the shooting. Like a scene in a melodrama, it played out in his mind. How Manning had worked his way up to where Fargo and the others stood. The way Manning had killed Huang Chow. For no reason. And the way Manning had insisted Huang Chow had murdered the man in Manning's mansion. Fargo now doubted that had happened, either. Manning had some reason to kill young Huang Chow. Fargo wished he knew what it was.

"I may need you to give testimony."

"I've got a family."

"Either that or give me the bullet."

"I can't—I'm sorry."

"Then how am I supposed to get rid of Manning and the others for you?"

"Everybody knows about you, Fargo. Knows how clever you are. You'll figure out a way."

Fargo smiled coldly. "I wish I had as much faith in me as you do."

Tomlinson gaped apprehensively at the door. "I need to be getting back. This is dangerous."

Tomlinson took the bullet from Fargo and slipped it into his trouser pocket. He'd made his point. Now it was up to Fargo to do the rest.

"Good night, Mr. Fargo."

"Good night, Tomlinson."

The small man slipped quietly out the door. Then he was only soft footfalls on the back stairs.

Fargo rolled himself a smoke and lay back on the bed and thought about what to do next. Confront Manning. That was the first thing. Somehow get another bullet from his gun. And then convince Tomlinson to testify as to the fact that the bullets were identical.

Fargo had just turned down the lamp, yawned, and was putting himself to bed when he heard the shot. A town this size, the shot could have come from anywhere. And the victim could be anybody. But Fargo knew better. Tomlinson had been shot and probably killed. He'd bet a considerable amount on that.

Somebody had followed him. And taken the bullet from him. And killed him.

It was too late to chase the killer. He'd be long gone by now.

But it wasn't too late to send a good thought out to the timid little man who'd helped him so much.

Fargo slept, but not well.

Fargo was up early, taking a cold bath in a tub and ambling over to a café for breakfast. The place was busy, smoky, and noisy. He sat at a table with two men he didn't know. There was nowhere else to sit. The single large room smelled of braised meat, fresh bread, and the latrine out back.

The two men talked privately, as if he wasn't there. The subject—and Fargo imagined that this was the subject at most of the tables—was the murders yesterday. The two men sounded most disturbed about Tomlinson.

"The way I got it," one of the workmen said, "is he had some kind of evidence against Manning and Manning had him killed."

"That's what I heard, too," his friend said.

"But we're right back where we started," the first man said. "Even with Duncan dead, Manning's still in charge. McGinley'll do what Manning tells him to do."

"Ain't no doubt about that."

Fargo was about halfway through his pancakes when he began to feel eyes on him. He eventually turned in his chair to find three men in business suits, their derbies placed on the table in a row, watching him and whispering comments to each other. He doubted they were saying nice things. Most likely, they'd heard about Manning's decree that Fargo was supposed to leave town and were speculating on why Fargo was stupid enough to still be here.

After the two workmen got up and left one of the three businessmen who'd been staring at him came over and sat down.

"You mind a little company?"

"Not if the company doesn't say anything to make me mad."

"Quite the contrary, Mr. Fargo. The company is going to make you an offer that could make you a very nice sum of money."

"How nice?"

He named a figure. "Is that nice enough for you?"

"I reckon that's nice enough for just about anybody."

"Jamison Recard," the man said, offering a long, slender hand that promised to be weak but was instead iron. Middle-aged, with a somber face belied by blue eyes that seemed amused by whatever they saw, Recard looked self-confident and friendly. "I own several ships that carry trade up and down the coast here. I've lived here for ten years and I've been very successful. My family and I like this place very much. There's just one problem. And I believe you met him—Del Manning."

Fargo laughed. "Oh, I met him, all right. He's probably got his deputies out looking for me right now. He told me to get out of town."

Recard did not laugh, only nodded somberly. Since the subject of Manning came up, Recard's blue eyes didn't look quite so merry. "The way you said 'his deputies' means that I don't have to explain to you the hold Manning has on this town."

"From what I can see, he runs it."

"That's exactly right. He runs it and we have to live under whatever law he decrees. Most of the time he leaves the merchants alone. But every once in a while he'll have his town council assess a tax that really cuts into our profits."

"And you put up with it?"

"Merchants who don't put up with it suddenly start not doing so well. Their buildings burn to the ground or they have a mysterious accident that leaves them in a wheelchair or some kind of really pernicious gossip about them starts making the rounds and they're forced to pack up their families and move away."

"Sounds like a bad deal."

Recard sat forward. "The sheriff was killed last night, as you know. McGinley isn't half as smart or clever as Duncan was. We think this is a perfect time to have a change of the guards—and to challenge Manning."

"And how do you do that?"

Recard slipped two fresh, good stogies from the breast pocket of his suit coat, offering one of them to Fargo. Fargo accepted. The only way you could survive in this place was to smoke in self-defense, cocoon yourself in your own haze.

As he lit up, Fargo glanced at the table where Recard had been sitting. His two cronies were watching them as avidly as they would a baseball game, back East, or an execution.

Recard, his own cigar also ablaze, puffed for a moment then said, "There've been a series of robberies in this area over the past six months. Duncan pretended that he was investigating them but we knew better."

"What kind of robberies?"

"Merchants, mostly. All the really expensive items they sell. Things that can be taken to San Fran, say, and be re-sold for good money."

"Any idea who's behind it?"

"Manning's behind it."

"Why would Manning get involved in something like that?"

Recard's smile was cold. "You have to understand

Mr. Manning, Fargo. He not only wants to rule over this town—he wants to rub your face in the fact that he's ruling over it. The whole economy on the coast took a turn for the worse a while back—a dry spell that lasted almost three years. A lot of merchants hereabouts were hurt pretty bad, including me. Still are, as a matter of fact. We balked at the last two taxes Manning tried to raise on us. Banded tight together and refused to pay them. So this is how Manning struck back."

"The robberies?"

"Absolutely. And they're just his style. He knows we know what he's up to but we can't prove it. That's what I mean about rubbing our faces in it." He hesitated. "But a few days ago he went too far. Several of us merchants decided to pull our money out of Manning's bank—it's the only one in town. We hid it in the attic of my store. Somebody slugged the man we had watching it at night and stole it. We know it was one of Manning's boys."

"How do you know that?"

"The servant Li Ping—he told us. He was a good man. We finally had a witness against Manning to take to court outside the county here. Then Manning killed Li Ping and blamed it on Huang Chow."

Fargo had no trouble believing any of this. He also understood now why Huang Chow was so adamant about not having killed Li Ping—because he hadn't. Manning had, so Li Ping couldn't testify against him.

"I take it Manning has your money?" Fargo said.

"He sure does. Without it, we can't pay our bills. And if we don't pay our bills, nobody will ship to us. And that means that before long, we'll all be out of business. We'll be forced to sell to Manning for a few cents on the dollar. Then this town'll be his lock, stock, and barrel." He looked at his friends at the table to left, then back at Fargo. "We want to hire you, Mr. Fargo. The night Li Ping came to us, he told us that he saw Manning stash all our money in his safe. We want you to steal our money back for us."

"I'm not a safecracker."

"That's not what I heard."

"If you mean, have I ever tricked a safe, yes. Am I an expert? No."

"We don't need an expert."

"You don't?"

"No. We have a slight advantage where this particular safe is concerned."

"And what would that be, Mr. Recard?"

"That would be, Mr. Fargo, the combination."

"You have the combination?"

"We sure do."

"Then why don't you just open it yourself?"

"Take a look at me, Mr. Fargo. And then take a look at my two friends. My eyesight is failing; Ron has gotten so bad he falls asleep while you're talking to him sometimes; and Allan is so nervous, he jumps when you sneeze. We're not exactly the kind of men you'd want to do a job like this. You still have to break into a house, you still have to get to the study, and you still have to get the money and get out without getting killed. This kind of job calls for a man of action, Mr. Fargo. And, I'm ashamed to say, that wouldn't be any of us."

"I'm afraid it wouldn't be me, either," Fargo said.

"That isn't the Skye Fargo they tell stories about."

"You're talking about the Skye Fargo who fought two grizzlies at the same time and won?"

"You're damned right I am."

"And the same Skye Fargo who was tied down to the desert with ropes but talked a buzzard into gnawing through the hemp for him?"

"That's the Skye Fargo we all love to hear about."

"And that's the Skye Fargo *I* love to hear about, too. I just wish those stories were true. I'd be one hell of a man if they were."

"You didn't fight two grizzlies at the same time?"

"Think it through, Mr. Recard. You know what one grizzly could do to a man? Well, then, think of what *two* grizzlies could do."

"And the same for the buzzard?"

"That would have to be one hell of a buzzard, Mr. Recard. A buzzard that not only understood English, but gave enough of a damn to listen."

"Are *any* of the stories true, Mr. Fargo?"

"Well, some of them, sure. I can handle myself pretty damned well, if I do say so myself. But two grizzlies and a buzzard that learned English? Afraid not." Fargo stood up. "Good luck with bringing Manning down. It's long past due."

He was gone before Recard could sputter out a final objection.

Fargo opened his hotel room door and a chunky man with breath so bad it could kill at twenty paces leaned into his line of vision and cracked Fargo across the skull with a child-sized ball bat. Just before his body had time to slam against the floor, Fargo's brain had time to figure out that the innocent-looking child-sized ball bat was lined with something that was likely lead. Then neither he nor his body nor his mind had time for anything except caving into darkness.

5

In the dream, a saintly woman dressed all in white
came and went in the room that was also white. He
tried to speak to her but couldn't, for some reason,
form words. Sometimes, there was a man with him,
an unlikely companion for her, a tobacco-chewing old
gink with a mean face and a filthy white shirt. He
always spoke to the woman but Fargo couldn't understand what he was saying. The words were garbled by
the massive chaw of tobacco in the old coot's mouth.

The dream seemed to last a long time. Hours and
hours. Maybe even days and days. Sometimes the
room was dark, sometimes it was bright, and sometimes the woman in white was tall and pink-
complexioned and sometimes she was short and of the
Mexican color. Unfortunately, the coot was the same
old bastard throughout.

Somewhere during all this a familiar female voice
asked, "Will he live?"

"We pray so," said a gentle female voice.

"Won't be no loss if he don't," said a gruff male
voice. The old coot and his wad of tobacco.

"We need to leave him alone now," said the gentle
female voice.

"I wish you'd let me stay in his room with him."

"It would be better if you didn't," said the other
woman.

There was pain—sometimes searing, numbing,
nearly unbearable pain—and there was memory. A

child's scrapbook of memories. Most of them sentimental but a few that were frightening.

And then a fresh memory—fresh as his confusion and occasional rage—a memory of men with clubs and the toes and heels of Texas boots kicking and stomping and stomping and kicking until he knew that he was bleeding from every part of his head—ears, eyes, nose, mouth. And still they stomped and kicked him. And there was laughter. And a bottle being passed around. And but a single thought now, that somehow someday he would kill these four men. If he survived, he would live for that reason only. To find them and kill them.

"You're a mean bastard," the elderly doc said around his wad of chaw.

"Thank you."

"You remember tryin' to take a swing at me?"

"Guess not."

"Try to help some miserable S.O.B. and he swings on ya."

"You want me to apologize?"

The doc giggled. "Nope. But I got a few patients haven't paid me in a long time and I was thinkin' about sendin' you to collect."

Fargo smiled but it hurt. They'd even stomped his face. "How long I been in here?"

"Nearly a week. You nearly went and died on us, Fargo. They sure did a hell of a job on you, let me tell you."

"I remember a couple of them."

"I reckon Manning sent them so it won't make any difference even if you *do* remember."

"Why not?"

"Why not?" The doc leaned over and spat at the floor. Fargo hoped there was a cuspidor somewhere in the vicinity of where the old fart was spitting. "Hell, Manning runs this town. You go bellyachin' to him—or McGinley—they'll run you out of town, which they plan to do as soon as you can walk, anyway." He tamped his chaw down with a finger to his cheek. "Like the time Huang Chow beat up Lala Huang. I didn't want her to go back home. Figured he'd do it again. Manning came here hisself and took her. Huang Chow was his favorite employee. He didn't want anything to upset him and make him less of a good employee."

"Huang Chow beat her up often?"

"Whenever he fell off the wagon and got drunk. This was back when they lived in a cottage right on Manning's estate. She finally moved into town here by herself."

Fargo felt a stab of pity for the young Chinese woman. Life was hard enough for her without an abusive brother. No wonder she lived alone. But when he thought of her loyalty to Huang Chow—love was the most difficult tie of all to break with somebody, even a brother who slapped you around.

"So Manning's still after me to leave town?"

"Soon as you can walk, I'm supposed to tell him. He says he'll have your horse outside and all ready to go. Between you and me, I think he thought you wouldn't live from the stomping you got. I had my doubts, too. And you're still pretty weak, Fargo."

"How long before I can get out of bed?"

The doc guffawed. "Oh, I reckon you can get out whenever you want to. But I'd put even money down sayin' you couldn't make it to the door."

"Even money, huh?"

The doc named his price.

"Hell, Doc, that'll be the easiest money I ever made."

"You think so, huh?"

"I know so."

"All right, Mr. Tough Guy. Get out of that bed and walk to the doorway over there."

Fargo figured the doc must be confusing him with somebody else. While not all the stories about the Trailsman were true—he had never, for instance, fought off an entire Indian tribe while continuing to chop wood for an elderly widow—Fargo knew that he was a cut above your average drifter. There could be no denying that. So walking to that doorway should be—

He eased himself out of bed, more slowly than he would have thought necessary. But the body wasn't doing what he ordered it to. Neither was his mind, for that matter. He had dancing red spots in front of his eyes. And he was dizzy.

A nurse peeked into the room and said, "Are you doin' it again, Doc?"

"This ain't none of your business, Madge."

"It's unseemly, you betting your patients they can't make it all the way to the door." She looked at Fargo and smiled. "Sometimes he bets patients they won't make it through his surgery."

Fargo laughed. The doc sounded mercenary and Fargo liked that. He hated pomposity and pretense. And the doc sure didn't indulge in either of those.

Fargo took mincing little steps, shocked that his legs refused to stiffen and fully support him. They were, in fact, trembling. He got a couple more steps and then fell right down in the middle of the floor.

"Told ya," Doc said.

Madge rushed in and got her arms around Fargo's chest and helped him to his feet. "I don't know how you live with yourself, Doc," she said. "Picking on poor, half-dead people like Mr. Fargo here."

"I'll try him again in a few days," the doc said. "Give him a chance to earn his money back."

She clucked about the doc's cynicism all the way over to the bed. She got Fargo laid out, tucked in, and brow wiped. He'd worked up a considerable sweat with that brief burst of exertion. "If you need anything, just ask for me."

"I appreciate that, Madge."

The doc said, "We got all your personal items up front in an envelope. You want me to take the bet you owe me out of that?"

Madge said, "That's disgusting."

"Sure, Doc," Fargo said, "long as you take only what you got coming."

"Why, my reputation is sterling, ain't it, Madge?" The doc winked at Fargo as he said it.

"Oh, yes," she said, "just sterling." And left the room.

It was two more days before Fargo, bored, cranky, filled exclusively with thoughts of repaying in kind the hurt that had been inflicted on him, decided to ask Nurse Madge to round up Doc and send him in.

"This is the day, huh?" Doc said when he came in.

"If you mean, is this the day I not only get out of bed but walk over to that doorway, you're damned right it is."

"Last fella that was as cocky as you ended up owin' me a lot of money."

"And I bet you spent it all on chaw."

"You got somethin' against chaw?"

"Only when the juice dribbles down your chin the way it does sometimes. Docs are supposed to be clean."

"You worry about fallin' on your ass again, Fargo, and I'll worry about my chin."

"Fair enough," Fargo said.

Fargo made a show of having a hard time getting out of bed. He groaned, he moaned, he even laid back down once, as if he were completely exhausted just from trying to sit up.

Doc said, "Maybe I should go take some of your money from your personal stuff now. Save me a trip later. You sure ain't gonna win this bet, Fargo."

"I'm not as strong as I was."

Doc giggled. Tobacco juice ran down his chin. "You're like that fella I was tellin' ya about. Cocky son, he was. Wouldn't listen to ole Doc that he wasn't ready to get out of bed yet. Got about halfway to the door here and fell right down in sech a way that he sprained his ankle. I almost hated to take his money."

"Yeah," Fargo said, "I'll bet you did."

"I'll tell you what, Fargo. You give up right now, call the bet off, and I'll just take *half* the money you bet."

"Let's write the pope and see if he'll make you a saint, Doc. You've got nothing but generosity in that heart of yours."

"Go ahead and make fun. I don't give a damn. That's a very generous offer. Otherwise, you'll try it again and fall down and maybe sprain your ankle like that other fella and then you'll owe me *all* of it."

At which point, Nurse Madge appeared in the doorway. "Aw, Lord, Doc, you takin' this poor man's money again?"

"Yep, and with pleasure. Him bein' so high and mighty and all. I say he ain't ready to get out of that bed. That's my considered opinion as a doc and if he won't take it, the hell with him. I'm happy to take his money."

"You shouldn't bet, Mr. Fargo," Nurse Madge said. "It says right in the Bible you shouldn't bet."

The Bible, Fargo thought. Never had a single simple principle—treat your neighbor as you'd like to be treated yourself—been perverted, twisted, distorted, and just plain lied about. People who professed to believe in the good book had no trouble cheating, robbing, maiming, and murdering each other and then braying on about how they lived by the golden rule. Any time somebody quoted—or misquoted—the Bible to him, Fargo wanted to reach for his gun.

"Thank you for that advice, Nurse Madge," Fargo said. "But if I don't get out of this bed and make it over to the doorway there, ole Doc here'll have another excuse to get into my personals and this time he'll probably rob me blind."

"Well, much as I wouldn't put that past him," Nurse Madge said, "I don't think it's a right thing for you to bet, Mr. Fargo."

And then he did it.

Leapt out of bed and hobbled one-legged over to the doorway, where he gave the surprised Nurse

Madge a quick kiss right on the lips. Then, favoring the other foot, he hobbled right back to bed and jumped back in.

"You cheatin' skunk," Doc said. "You made me think you were still ailin' bad."

"That's right, Doc. And you were all ready to take advantage of my ailin'."

Nurse Madge frowned in disgust and waved a dismissive hand at them. "You're both goin' to hell, the way you abuse the good book."

Shaking his head with great theatrical sorrow, Doc said, "And here I thought you was an honest and upright man, Fargo. I am deeply disappointed."

Fargo laughed. "You'd better get out of here, Doc, before you get me to cryin' tears of remorse and shame."

The doc cussed, spat, and then left the room.

6

The first place Fargo went was to his hotel room for a bath and clean clothes. Moving very quickly still hurt him some but he was beginning to feel strong again. Shaved, all shined up, and sheathed in a clean pair of buckskins and his trusty boots, he walked the street to Recard's place of business, a haberdashery that was pretty damned imposing once you got past the drab exterior. The place was fragrant with the scents of new clothes, good tobacco, and expensive leather goods.

Both Recard and his clerk were busy with customers so Fargo walked around and looked at what there was to be had. Nice as these new clothes were, they did put a lot of burden on a man to stay out of gunfights, knife fights, whip fights, fights on the ground, fights in the water, fights in the snow, fights up against the sides of buildings, and fights in areas where horses had recently dropped fresh road apples. New clothes, when you came right down to it, had a way of inhibiting a man's way of life.

The dude Recard was waiting on obviously didn't feel the same way. He bought top-of-the-line everything, including a purple pair of drawers that could get you hanged if anybody ever found out you were wearing them. He even, as the final affront to masculinity, bought a top hat. Now just what the hell kind of so-called man bought purple drawers *and* a top hat? And just where could a so-called man wear such things? And what kind of world was this getting to be anyway where such things went on?

Fargo fell asleep in a leather chair. He was awakened when Recard said, "You snore pretty loud, Mr. Fargo." They were in the back of the store, no one around. Still, Recard spoke quietly.

"You should hear me fart."

Recard looked as if he didn't quite know how to take that. He said, "I stopped by to see you a couple of times but you were unconscious."

"I appreciate that."

"I suppose you need some new clothes after the way they worked you over." He said this as he looked over Fargo's attire and clearly found it wanting.

"That isn't why I'm here."

"No?"

"No. I'm ready to take on that job you talked about."

"You are?" Disbelief edged his tone of voice. "After what they did to you, I assumed you'd want to put as much distance as you could between you and this town."

"I'm going to take care of every one of them. And I'm going to take care of Manning while I'm at it."

Recard's happiness showed in both his eyes and his voice. "The other merchants are going to be very happy to hear about this, believe me. When can you get started?"

"Today. I'm going to ride out and see Manning right now, in fact."

"See Manning? My Lord, you must be crazy. Don't you know what he'll do to you?"

"Maybe he won't. Not after I tell him that I want to work for him."

"Work for him?"

Fargo levered himself out of the deep chair. Pain dispersed itself throughout his body. Thank God he was mad. Mad could overcome just about any kind of pain you ever experienced. Mad was better than whis-

42

key in certain circumstances. And mad never left you hungover either.

"You think of a better way to get into his house, Recard? Plus, he's in need of a man. He lost Huang Chow and the man he accused Huang Chow of killing."

Recard sounded hesitant about this. "What if he asks you to burn down our businesses? That's the next step. He's got our money and he still hasn't run us out. You can bet he'll want to up the ante."

"Well," Fargo said, smiling. "As a loyal employee, I guess I won't have any choice but to burn your buildings down, now will I, Mr. Recard?"

He gave a little salute off the edge of his hat and left the store.

Sheriff McGinley, wearing a suit instead of his deputy duds, jerked several inches up from his chair when the front door opened and Fargo walked in.

Fargo was pleased with the reaction. McGinley would've reacted about the same way if he'd seen a corpse come strolling through his door. "Sit down, McGinley," he said. "I'm not going to put any hurt on you just yet. So you can relax for a couple of days."

"You're threatening a duly appointed high sheriff?"

Fargo smiled. "I never thought of it that way. But I guess I am."

McGinley, who was back in control of himself, picked up a fresh cigar and pointed it like a bullet at the door. "I'm going to do you a favor, Fargo. You walk out of that door right now, you ride straight out of town as fast as that horse of yours will take you, and I won't arrest you."

Fargo walked over and helped himself to a cup of coffee from the pot on the stove. "You arrest people for getting beaten up in this town?"

"We do if they're wanted by the law."

Fargo sipped his coffee and walked back to McGinley's desk. "Those deputies of yours around?"

"They're doing their jobs, if that's what you mean."

"They led the charge."

"What charge?"

"When they beat me to death last week. Or thought they had. And they should have. Because now I'm going to return the favor."

"You sure do like to make threats, Fargo."

Fargo had some more coffee. "You seen Manning yet today?"

"Far as I know, he's out to his ranch. He only comes to town a few days a week. Why?"

The door opened and in came one of the deputies who'd beaten him. The long, sinewy man with the long, scowling face reacted just about the same way McGinley had. As if he was looking at a corpse. The man had also been at the attempted lynching of Huang Chow. An all-around model citizen.

McGinley smiled. "Mr. Fargo here don't like you, Cliff."

"What the hell's he doing here?" Cliff said.

"Near as I can figure out, he came in to pass along his threat. He claims that you and the other boys tried to beat him to death."

"The hell we did."

McGinley said, "He's tough, Mr. Fargo is. But you know what? I don't think he's as tough as he thinks he is. Give him a little taste of your right hand, Cliff." McGinley, eyes twinkling, amused, said to Fargo, "He wins the boxing matches every year at the county fair. He even holds his own against the professionals."

"I guess I'd better get out of here," Fargo said, "tough hombre like that being here and all."

"You don't think he's tough?" McGinley said of the man in the fancy black shirt and trousers who carried a Colt with a barrel half as long as his leg. "Show him, Cliff."

"Yeah," Fargo said, "c'mon on and show me, Cliff."

He literally felt dizzy with rage. He was getting an opportunity to bust up one of the men who'd damned

44

near killed him. And Fargo hadn't been out of the sickbed for much more than an hour yet.

Fargo put down his tin cup of coffee. "C'mon, show me, Cliff," he said again.

Cliff wouldn't meet his eye. Finally he said, "It's too early for a fight."

"This isn't going to be a fight, Cliff," Fargo said. "This is going to be a stomping. I've still got busted ribs because of you and your friends. And I'm going to see to it that you feel the same, too. And, hell, Cliff, it's *never* too early for a fight."

He moved toward Cliff. Cliff backed to the door. Found the door handle. Opened it. "I haven't made my rounds yet, this morning, Sheriff. Maybe I'd best do that now."

"Cliff's pretty scary," Fargo said to McGinley. "I can see why you put so much stock in him."

"Shut up, Fargo."

Fargo flared at Cliff. "Sometime in the next twenty-four hours I'm going to find you and put you in the hospital. About the only way you can avoid it is to pack up your things and get out of town. Tell that to your friends, too."

"Hey," McGinley said, "you don't run people out of town, I do."

"Oh, yeah, right," Fargo said. "I forgot. You're the high sheriff of the county."

He was upon Cliff before Cliff even had time to flinch, let alone flee. Fargo grabbed the man by his shirt and the seat of the pants and then fired him out the front door on to the dusty street. Citizens sure didn't like to see their law enforcement officers pitched out. Undermined a fella's faith in his sheriff's department.

"See you around, McGinley," Fargo said. "Real soon now."

Then he walked out through the open door to the street where Cliff was just starting to pick himself up. "Like I said, Cliff, it's never too early for a fight."

*　　*　　*

45

Fargo made friends everywhere he went that day.

As he halted his stallion in front of the iron gates that closed off Manning's huge manor house—the ranch with its bunkhouses and barns and corrals lay half a mile from here—two men with shotguns emerged from a small guard house. One pointed his shotgun right at Fargo's head while the other walked up to the Ovaro stallion.

"You got business here?"

"I sure do." Fargo had learned that if you always sounded confident, people tended to believe your lies.

"Yeah? What kind of business?"

"For that, you'd have to ask Mr. Manning. He told me to stop out today."

"What's your name?"

"Fargo."

His name and presence sure had a peculiar effect on people in these parts. The guard's eyes narrowed and his large head gave a start. "Fargo? He hates you."

"Correction. He *used* to hate me. Now he's thinking of hiring me."

"Now there's a crock," said the other guard.

But Fargo could see that the guard nearer him was getting nervous. He wouldn't want to turn away a man with a legitimate appointment to see Mr. Manning would he? And the story about maybe hiring him was so odd it just had to be true.

The guard said, "Let me get my horse and I'll take you up to the house."

"Shoot the bastard, I say," the other guard said. "He's lyin'."

"If he's lyin', I'll shoot him when I get him up to the house."

"Let's just shoot him right here."

"I hate to be late for my appointment," Fargo said. "Especially if I have to tell Mr. Manning that the reason I'm late was because of you two."

"I guess he's right there," the first guard said. He walked bowlegged over to a ground-tied and saddled pinto and heaved his considerable carcass upward. "Follow me," he said to Fargo.

The other guard sighted along the barrel of his shotgun, obviously pleasuring himself with an image of Fargo's head exploding in three or four big, bloody chunks.

"Get the gate, Lem," the guard on the horse said.

"I still say we should shoot him here."

"Just get the gate and shut up."

Lem, the poor soul, looked disappointed as all hell that he wouldn't get to disintegrate Fargo's head. He made a pouty face like that of a spoiled child then finally brought his shotgun down and opened the gate. Lem said, "Hope Mr. Manning kicks his ass, Pete."

"We'll have to wait and see."

Pete was apparently a frustrated tour guide and expected every one of the people he escorted up to the mansion to provide the appropriate number of oohs and aahs. He told a profoundly disinterested Fargo how much the place cost, how many rooms it had in it, how there was some interior stuff that had been imported from France, how there was a chandelier that you could see from a half mile away on a clear night, and how very important people visited here regularly.

"Am I one of those important people?" Fargo said.

Pete the tour guide didn't even smile. In fact, he glowered. "You got guts, Fargo, I'll give you that. But you never dealt with a man like Mr. Manning before. He decides to dislike you, he can make your life so miserable you'd rather get captured by Indians and fried for dinner."

The manor-style house was dramatic, Fargo had to give it that. It looked like an illustration in one of those ladies' books where the heroine, beautiful and fragile, dressed in a flowing gown, ran down the plantationlike front steps in fear of something monstrous that was chasing her from the house. Fargo was in hopes that a beautiful woman—forget frail, buxom would be nice right now—would put in an appearance.

A servant in livery stood in front of the massive oak front door and swung it back as Pete and Fargo approached. A maid in a severe black dress, which did nothing to hide the pleasing push of her large breasts, greeted Fargo and took his hat. He wished for a moment that the chapeau wasn't so sweated. He liked to do everything he could to get women of the large breasted persuasion to admire him.

Pete started up his tour guide routine as they walked down a parquet-floored hall that was as filled with artwork of various kinds and styles as a museum.

"I'll have to show you my hotel room sometime, Pete," Fargo said. "There're some interesting teeth marks on the floor. I'm pretty sure they're from rats. Big ones."

Again, no smile from Pete.

Pete knocked, a deep voice far on the other side of the door said something unintelligible that Pete obviously took for permission to enter, and the two men went inside.

The pope would have envied this den.

First of all, it was big enough to hide an army in. Second of all, the three genuine Persian rugs covering the hardwood floors would probably be worth enough to ransom several kings and all their mistresses. And third of all, even with the vast globe, the floor-to-ceiling library, and the extensive art collection depicting fancy boy English gents riding to hounds and walking around with riding crops shoved up their arses (not really but they certainly did look stiff, those Brits)—even with all the priceless, outsized, and dazzling things that captured Fargo's eyes—the most compelling of all was Manning's desk. It seemed as if enough wood had gone into its making to build a wagon, with a pile left over to keep the fire hot for days.

Manning was dandied up to look pretty much like the Brits in the paintings. Fargo did not care to speculate where the man was keeping his riding crop.

Manning said, "It won't do you any good, Fargo."

"What won't do me any good?"

"Trying to get permission to stay in my town."

"That's not why I'm here."

Pete said, "You want me to stay, Mr. Manning?"

"Wait out in the hall."

"Yessir."

"And keep your gun handy. I may ask you to shoot Fargo here."

"That'd be my pleasure, sir." He left.

"All right if I sit down?" Fargo said.

"No."

"You going to offer me a drink?"

"Don't be ridiculous."

"How about introducing me to your maid?"

Manning had about as much a sense of humor as Pete. "Just what the hell are you doing here, Fargo?"

"Asking for a job."

"A what?"

"A job. You know who I am and what I can do. I can outfight and outshoot any man on your ranch."

"What a charming streak of modesty you have."

"I'm not saying I'm great. I'm saying they're not very good."

"Yes, well, you should see Pete shoot at a target sometime."

"He do that in addition to being a tour guide for this place?"

"He happens to be proud to work in such a place. That's a sign of loyalty, something I doubt you'd understand." He stood up. And up with him came that special-made gun of his. The one that proved he'd killed Huang Chow. "I want you to leave. And I don't mean just my estate. I mean leave town. I'm giving shoot-to-kill orders at sundown. I'm also going to offer a five hundred dollar reward to anybody who kills you. That change your mind about leaving, Fargo?"

"I still wish you'd introduce me to that maid of yours, Manning. She's something special."

Manning thumbed back the hammer on his weapon. "Get out."

"You try and be nice to people and look what you get."

But Fargo figured he'd probably pushed the situation about as far as he could. Manning might actually shoot him. He owned the town, including the sheriff and the judge. Who would question him if he did kill Fargo?

Fargo nodded, walked over to the huge globe, and gave it a spin so violent it rocked on its wooden mounting. He half-expected to get a bullet in the back.

On his way out, he made sure to smile pretty at the maid as she handed him his hat. She smiled pretty right back. He'd finally found somebody in this place with a sense of humor. He pried his eyeballs off her breasts and left, Pete being nowhere to be found.

7

In town, Fargo went to Lala Huang's. He was about to knock when he heard voices. Or thought he did. He knocked. But when she came to the door, she invited him in. It didn't take long to see that she was the only person there. Hearing voices was not a good thing, Fargo decided. He might've been punched in the head one time too many.

The smells of strong tea and Chinese cooking made him realize that nearly every household in the West held strong odors of one ethnic group or another. German, Italian, Irish households were easy to tell apart just by scents alone.

Even in a white blouse and dungarees, she was stamped with her Chinese ancestry—a frail butterfly. "This West of yours—it is so complicated sometimes."

"Listen carefully. Manning has a special gun."

"Special?"

"Made just for him. You with me so far?"

"Yes, I think so."

"Well, I was told that when Martin extracted the bullet from this servant—the bullet that Manning said belonged to your brother's gun—it was Manning's bullet."

"Then Manning—" He could see the excitement in her face. Even though her brother was dead, for him to be vindicated would give her great pleasure and esteem among her own people. He had died innocent, as she had insisted all along.

"It won't be that easy," Fargo said. "All Manning has to do is to claim that Huang Chow took Manning's gun and used it for the murder. To make it look as if Manning did it."

"But who would believe that?"

"Doesn't matter who'd believe it. Nobody in town is going to be listened to if Manning says Huang Chow killed the man."

"Manning murdered Huang Chow in cold blood."

"Yes, he did."

"So that the real truth would not come out."

Fargo nodded again. "That's right."

"But what can we do?" Her small face was a mask of frustration. "He must be brought to justice. There is so much talk in this West of yours about justice, Fargo. But so few receive it. If you go up against the rich and powerful as my brother did—you see what happens."

For the first time, he recognized a strong scent of lilac. Perfume. He was surprised to find her wearing it. She seemed to shun the cosmetic ways of town women. She had to know how beautiful she was without any help at all. He said, "I need to know something from you."

"What?"

"I'm told that Huang Chow beat you. I need to know the truth."

She dropped her gaze, embarrassed. "Another thing about your West, Fargo. People tell each other everything. There is very little that is held private. My brother—sometimes when he drank, he would come home and hit me. Why is this so important to you?"

"How often did he drink?"

"I wish we would not speak of this, Fargo. It darkens his reputation and he is not here to speak up for himself. Many men in your West drink and beat their wives. Huang had a sister instead."

"What I'm trying to figure out is how much Manning would have trusted him. If he was drunk a lot,

52

Manning probably wouldn't have taken him into his confidence."

"I see."

"So did he drink a lot?"

"Yes. And he was the only Chinese man in the area who did. He brought dishonor to our name. But I felt sorry for him. Many times, he tried to stop. He even had me lock him in this little home of mine. Not let him out for several days. He hoped to cure himself this way. He stayed here five days. I did not have the heart to keep him locked up any more than that. He was fine for a week or so. Manning let him come back to work—Manning was always firing him for his drinking—and things were good for a few weeks. Then something happened—and he changed."

"He started drinking again?"

"No—not right away. He—learned something, he said. He said that he was going to get a lot of money and that we were going to move away from here."

The obvious answer wasn't always the correct one, but Fargo thought that here his instinct was probably right on the money—the money that Manning had stolen from the merchants. Somehow, Huang Chow had learned of this. Somehow, he'd also learned the combination to the safe. He might well have been stealing the money—but where did the dead servant fit in? Maybe what Fargo had come up with was *half* an easy answer. He sensed that the second half was going to be a lot tougher to find out than the first.

"But you never figured out where he was going to get the money?"

"No. He only told me this two days before he died. We really didn't get a chance to talk in private again. But I did not want this money, anyway."

"Why not?"

"Because it was trouble money, Fargo. Huang had yearned all his life to be an important man and he was ready to do anything to become that—where else would my brother find such money? He would put us all in danger to get it. No other way was possible. We can barely eke out a living. But here he was talking of living in fancy hotels in San Francisco and buying me silk dresses." The tears were bittersweet—she'd obviously loved him and yet he'd been for her a constant source of frustration, fear, and heartbreak. "A big man, a big man." She said this scornfully between sobs.

Fargo stood up and walked over to her and kissed her on the forehead. The scent of lilacs was strong on her. He took her hand and said, "I'm going to figure this all out for you—and me. Then I'm going after the men who tried to kill me."

"You're brave, Fargo," she said, smiling at him with glassy eyes.

"Or stupid."

"But isn't that a part of bravery, Fargo? Stupidity, I mean?"

He laughed. "You may have a point there."

And then he took her slight body in his arms. He was half-afraid he might hurt her. Beauty and the beast. Her bones so fine he could crush them at will. But he wasn't thinking of crushing her, of course. He was thinking of bedding her.

His lips found hers and in that instant his desire ignited. Their tongues exchanged invisible fire and he felt his hardness pressed against the delicate shape of her stomach.

He swept her up in his arms and carried her over to the bed. After laying her down, he bent down and began removing her clothes as their mouths fumbled after each other with blinding need.

He first concentrated on the nipples beneath the soft fabric of her shirt. He rubbed them between thumb and forefinger until she began to undulate on the bed, her hips finding a sexual rhythm that caused him to slide his hand down between her legs and ease its way to the damp warmth he could feel pressed against the fabric of her dungarees.

It was less than a minute later that he was sliding

those dungarees over her hips and down the slender elegance of her legs. He turned her slightly toward him so that he could use his mouth to bring her to the ultimate ecstacy.

He worked skillfully, sharing her pleasure as her cries got louder and louder. And when she reached completion once, twice, three times, he slid his own pants down and eased himself into her.

She reached down as they were making love and took his large, hard presence in her delicate fingers, exciting him ever higher. Their mouths were savage to each other at this point. The nails of her free hand raked his back as he drover deeper and deeper, faster and faster into her. She bucked against him, surprisingly strong for her size.

He was just leaving Lala Huang's when he saw Recard talking to a man in the middle of the street. The man pointed at Fargo and Recard swung his head around. He waved Fargo over.

"This is Frank Heilbronner," Recard said. "He owns the apothecary. Sells the most honest drugs in the whole state."

Heilbronner, a thick-bodied, balding man, smiled. "Except for the whiskey. I have to buy the same bilge everybody else does."

"An apothecary that sells whiskey?" Fargo said wryly. "I'm shocked."

"About ninety-eight percent of every medicine we sell is booze," Heilbronner said.

"So did you go out and see Manning?" Recard said, getting back to business. "And by the way, it's all right to talk in front of Frank. He's one of the merchants Manning stole from."

Fargo nodded. "Yes, I did."

"How'd it go."

"About like I expected."

Recard frowned. "Why don't you tell us what happened, Fargo, instead of making us guess?"

"Because if I tell you what happened, you'll think

I didn't have any luck. But things went about the way I figured they would."

"Meaning what?"

"Meaning he threatened me and threw me out."

Heilbronner glowered at Recard. "I thought you said that Fargo here knew what he was doing."

"Well, I guess I was wrong."

Fargo laughed. "I know this is probably irritating, gentlemen. But I don't know who I can trust and who I can't. So the next part of my plan has to stay private for the time being."

"You can trust Heilbronner just fine, Fargo."

"And how about you, Recard? I don't know much more about you than I do Heilbronner. What if you're secretly working for Manning and making all these merchants think you're on their side?"

"I resent that, Fargo. In fact, I ought to fire you right now."

"I wasn't accusing you of anything, Recard. I was just saying that I need to be careful. You'll know by sundown if my plan works or not."

"*How* will we know, Mr. Fargo?" Heilbronner said.

Fargo smiled. "Well, if you find me residing in a long box over at the funeral parlor you'll know it didn't."

"You seem to find this very amusing," Recard said.

"You will, too, Recard, if I can pull it off. Pretty good plan, if I do say so myself."

"How good can it be if you get killed?" Heilbronner said.

"No plan's foolproof, Mr. Heilbronner. But I'm sure going to try and make this one as close as possible. The money Recard offered me is good but not that good. I've got a few ladies I'd like to look up and a few poker games I'd like to sit in on. I'm not in any hurry to die." He offered each man his hand and said, "I wish us all good luck, gentlemen."

And then walked away.

* * *

Just after dusk, Fargo angled himself through the barbed wire fence on the east edge of Manning's estate. The house was less than four hundred yards away, but he had had to wait for the sentry to ride past. The Trailsman knew he had only a few minutes before the man would circle back again.

The huge manor house gleamed with light. The chandelier that seemed to be the centerpiece of the elegant home was like a sunburst through the windows. Out front, a large round pool housed elegant swans.

Fargo raced to a giant oak tree, hiding behind it. A guard stood at the rear entrance of the house. He carried a rifle over his shoulder like a soldier. He didn't move away from the rear door. Fargo would have to take care of him without making any noise. No gunshots, that was for sure.

He needed a way to distract the guard and groped around on the ground until he found a suitable rock. Fargo had a good throwing arm. He was able to get his body into it and throw with both power and accuracy. This would be the true test. If he could take the guard out before the guard had a chance to fire on him, he'd be all right. Otherwise—

Night settled in, the stars sharp in the sky; lonesome dogs cried out before giving up the day and surrendering to sleep; the distant bunkhouse was alive with the harsh laughter of men without women.

How best to distract the guard?

He decided the easiest way would be to throw two rocks instead of one. Aim the first at the gazebo off to the right and when the guard moved to see what had caused the noise, hurl the second rock at his head.

The gazebo rock was no trouble. The guard did exactly what Fargo had hoped he would do. He turned and started in the direction of the gazebo. The problem being for Fargo that between the gloom and the movement, the guard wasn't the cleanest target. Fargo had to risk rushing toward the man, whose hat also presented a problem. The hat might deflect the direct impact of the rock. Fargo had to aim low enough and hard enough to drop the man with a single throw.

The sound of the rock thunking the guard's head was almost as loud as the sound of the rock against the gazebo had been. Fargo rushed the man, wanting to make sure he was unconscious. Fargo's momentary concern that maybe he'd struck the man too hard—perhaps killed him—vanished when Fargo knelt down next to him and saw that he was one of the men who'd beaten him so badly. Regardless, the man was out for sure. That was all Fargo cared about.

Fargo hurried to the back door and slipped inside.

The smells of the kitchen—Mexican food well-prepared—gave him momentary hunger pangs. He tiptoed up the three stone steps leading to the kitchen. The room was huge. A lone Mexican woman stood at one of two stoves, using a long wooden spoon to stir a pan most likely filled with sauce. She sang a merry song in her native tongue as she worked. He needed to move quickly but there was no way he was going to hurt a woman. He would have to wait her out, hoping she would have a reason to go into the dining room very soon.

His biggest worry was that somebody would find the guard and know that something was wrong inside. Despite the legend and the myth, the Trailsman was not superhuman. There were likely four or five guards close by the house. After knocking out the guard and sneaking into the mansion, Fargo would be fair game for any one or all of them.

The Mexican cook took a plate of beans into the dining room.

Fargo was only seconds behind her.

There were eight people at the long table. Manning sat in a chair, his back to the kitchen door. Fargo's gaze fell first on Manning's wife. While the other people at the table all showed shock and fear, an insolent smile touched her provocative lips. This was a woman who truly detested her husband.

Fargo wasted no time.

He pushed the barrel of his Colt against the back of Manning's head and said, "Stand up. We're going into your den and have a talk."

He looked at Manning's guests. "I advise you against rounding up any of the guards. If anybody tries to get in the den, I'll kill Manning on the spot. Understand me?"

The guests nodded coldly, hating him, terrified of him.

All but Mrs. Manning. The insolent smile was now an outright smirk. She was apparently having a grand old time watching her husband—her all-powerful husband—being humiliated this way.

"Let's go, Manning," he said.

"You think I don't know what you're up to, Fargo?"

"Go ahead and tell me."

They were locked in the large study. Fargo knew that in moments, some of Manning's men would begin their assault on the room. Fargo would, if he was them. They'd distract him by pounding on the door—and then make some attempt to come through one of the windows. There was a skylight. Maybe they'd even try that.

"You want me to hire you."

"That's a very good guess," Fargo said, impressed, in spite of himself, by the man's understanding of the situation.

"You wanted to show me how bad my men are at protecting me. And once you'd shown me, you wanted me to say there's only one man who could really protect me and that's our good friend Fargo."

The first knock came on the door. Followed by a gruff, unfamiliar male voice. "No matter what you do, you'll never get out of that room alive, Fargo. Give up now and we'll let you walk away. Isn't that right, Mr. Manning?"

Manning seemed unfazed by Fargo. He said, quite

calmly, "I can handle this situation by myself. There's no reason to get Fargo mad. He might do something that both of us would regret, so please go back to what you were doing."

Something was wrong, Fargo knew. You knock out a man's guards, burst into his house and force him at gunpoint into his den—and then he not only acts calmly, he also refuses to let his own men help him.

Fargo took a few steps back so that he could glance around the den without Manning jumping him. There was no other light except that provided by the fireplace. The flames were low. The fire needed a few new logs. The flames filled the room with looming shadows, shadows so deep that somebody crouched behind a chair, say, wouldn't have any trouble concealing himself. Fargo glimpsed every section of the room he could. Leather sofa, matching chairs, the dry bar—there could be someone anywhere. Was this why Manning was acting so brave, almost amused? Did he have a guard hidden somewhere in the room?

"There's one thing wrong with your plan, Fargo," Manning said. "What would I get out of hiring you? You're good but you're not infallible. Somebody could kill you and get to me. So in that sense, I don't gain anything but firing the guards I already have, even though you did an excellent job of getting past them tonight." The man's demeanor was so casual it grated on Fargo. Was this man so sure of himself that not even Fargo's gun could put fear in his eyes? "Then there's the other problem. You're not here because you want to save my life. You're not even here because I pay a good wage. You're here because you want to prove that I murdered Huang Chow and Li Ping for my own purposes. And on top of it you want to be close enough to the four men you allege beat you—so you can pay them back one at a time." A superior smile. "Any of this sound familiar, Fargo?"

By this time, the knocking on the door had become

a pounding. Fargo knew that someone was hiding in the den. "Who's here, Manning? With us?"

"What in the devil are you talking about?"

Either the man was one hell of a good actor—one who should be on a New York stage—or he really didn't know that there was somebody else in the den.

"What do you mean?"

"You don't sense somebody here—besides us?"

"I don't know what you're talking about," Manning said. And he genuinely sounded as if he didn't.

"You may need me more than you think, Manning. There's somebody in this room."

"That's ridiculous. We'd know it by now."

"Oh?" Fargo said. "Maybe or maybe not. But I've got good instincts and I'm sure I'm right."

A new voice: "Open this door, Fargo, or we won't show you any mercy when we finally get our hands on you."

"My uncle," Manning said. A few minutes ago, he would have sounded amused by all the fuss people were making about him being pushed to the den at gunpoint. But he had to strain to sound amused now. Fargo could see Manning's eyes begin to search the room. He saw his face tighten as his eyes confronted the deep shadows. He saw him begin to bite his lip as every tiny sound the house made took on significance. Funny how a room could change when you believed the possibility that somebody was hiding in it. Funny how a room you spent time in every day could suddenly look alien, menacing, filled not only with shadow but the possibility of death.

"You really think somebody's in here, Fargo?"

"Yes."

"Then I'm going to hire you." His voice was tight, fearful now. Manning seemed to know something he wasn't sharing with Fargo. "There's a thousand dollars in it if you can get me out of this room alive."

"What the hell're you talking about, Manning? All we need to do is walk to the door."

Manning's terror was apparently spreading. He found the hair on the back of his neck starting to bristle. He found himself—absurdly—staring into the fireplace, as if somebody could be hiding there.

And then it happened. Without so much as a whisper of sound somebody came up from behind Fargo and slammed him so hard across the back of the head that he started to black out immediately.

Two gunshots fired, the last thing Fargo heard before losing consciousness.

Somebody had been hiding behind a tall leather chair that sat next to an end table and a kerosene lamp. Somebody who'd suddenly crossed the room, knocked out Fargo and shot Manning.

Then there was darkness. A deep chasm that consumed Fargo as he felt himself falling, faster, faster. . . .

Pain and confusion enveloped him before the darkness started to lift—

There was a pounding on the door.

Fargo pushed against the floor, still not completely conscious, knowing instinctively that he was in a dangerous situation. A part of his mind had already worked out the predicament he was in. And even before he was quite steady on his feet, his eyes confirmed what his mind had speculated.

Manning lay unmoving on the floor. The two bullets had already loosed heavy, swirling amounts of blood from his wounds. The way his eyes stared dumb and panic-stricken at the ceiling, Fargo had no doubt he was dead.

There was also something else he had no doubt of. He bent and grabbed his Colt. Put the edge of its barrel to his nose. Whoever the killer had been, he'd used Fargo's own gun.

The shooter.

So there had been someone in the room, just as Fargo had sensed. Fargo jammed his gun into his holster and began a desperate search of the den. He looked behind every chair, both couches, even a closet near the back of the long room. And nothing. Where the hell had the man been hiding? And how the hell had he gotten away?

That was when he heard somebody shout: "Stand back! We're going to break the door down!"

Fargo ran to one of the mullioned windows. As he'd assumed, a mob of men waited there to grab him. He'd likely be killed on the spot once they learned that Manning was dead. Manning was their paymaster, a very important hombre in their world.

Just then the fireplace crackled and instantly he figured out his one last chance of escape. He rushed to the fireplace where he found a metal can of oil kerosene used to set the fire blazing. He grabbed the can and ran around the room, dousing every surface he could find. He knew he had only seconds. Whatever they were using to batter the door down, it was working. The heavy oak was starting to give and crack. He had only seconds.

He grabbed pieces of newspaper and jabbed them into the flames. He took the fiery paper and followed the path he'd made with the kerosene. In moments, the entire room was ablaze, flames reaching as high as the ceiling, fanning out everywhere.

Fargo raced to the door that was now being reduced to splinters. His only hope was to hide off to the side of the doorway, wait until all the men at the door rushed in, and then to sneak out into the hall.

What he hadn't counted on was the speed of the fire. The room was already heavy with gray smoke, behind which he could see and hear crackling flames. He dropped to his knees, jerked a red bandana from his back pocket, and covered his nose and mouth. Could he hold out till the door was broken through?

Eyes stinging, lungs starting to hurt, he worried now that he'd have to open the door and surrender himself. He sure didn't want to die in a fire. He'd seen that happen to other men. It was a horrible way to cross into the next world.

The door popped open and was immediately slammed to the floor.

"Start bringing buckets of water!" someone shouted. The footsteps of at least half a dozen men pounded on the hallway floor.

Weak from inhaling smoke, his mind seemed to capsize every few seconds. Fargo scrambled to his feet. Deep inside the gray smoke that now escaped the den and began to fill the hallway, the shape of a man stood—a silhouette. Didn't matter who it was or what he was doing. This was the first of many men Fargo would have to defeat to escape from the house.

He hurled himself at the shape. Within seconds, the shape became human, bone, flesh, clothing. Fargo grabbed the man around the neck and slammed his head against the doorframe. The shape slipped to the floor, unconscious.

Fargo jumped over him and started down the hall in the opposite direction from which he and Manning had come. He was able to outrun the smoke, though to do so he had to bring even more of the stuff into his heaving lungs. The hallway came to a "T." Which direction? His question was answered quickly for him. From the left came three men, each carrying two buckets of sloshing water. When they saw him, one of them shouted his name.

Fargo ran in the opposite direction, his Colt drawn. A glance over his shoulder told him that two of the men who'd beaten him were now chasing him. They were firing at him but given the density of the smoke and the fact that they were running, their shots were wild.

Fargo turned around completely, facing them, taking his time to make sure his shots counted. And they did. He heard one, then two bodies, thumping against the floor. One of the men cried "I'm shot!" There was only silence from the other one.

Fargo ran on. He had only one thought, now. Get to his horse. By the time he reached the back door, he heard more and more people trampling into the house through the front doors, no doubt bringing buckets of water. This meant he'd have few guards—if any—to stop him when he got to his stallion.

He walked in a crouch, gun ready, along the side of the house. He had the sense—because a lot of the shouting had died down—that maybe the fire was being brought under control. He had to hurry.

There was a bucket brigade stretching from the large swan pool to the house. In all the rush, none of Manning's men seemed to notice Fargo, sweeping wide now, trying to become invisible in the darkness on the edge of the lawn. Or so he thought. A man dove at Fargo just as he reached his horse. The man had him around the neck in a strong, deadly lock. Fargo had no doubt the man was capable of breaking his neck or choking him to death. Fargo lanced an elbow into the man's rib cage. He knew the man felt it because the grip on Fargo's neck slipped slightly. Fargo took advantage of the moment by stomping down so hard on the man's arch that the man's grip loosened even more. The man was about to shout for help when Fargo spun around and smashed the man's face so hard that he broke four teeth in the process. Fargo then brought his knee up into the man's crotch. And in case that wasn't enough, Fargo clubbed the man on the right temple. The man's eyes rolled back in his head as he fell over backward, with nothing to break his fall.

But Fargo wasn't done fighting yet.

As if on cue, a man from behind him and a man from somewhere ahead of him began firing rifles at him. Fargo jerked the reins of his magnificent horse and started riding toward the darkness in the east. The bullets flying past him were becoming tougher and tougher to avoid. He leaned forward, wrapped his arms around the neck of his animal, and made ready for a jump over a wire fence that was approximately waist-high.

The stallion didn't have any trouble with the jump but it did have trouble with the next two men who bolted from the bunkhouse and started chasing after Fargo with their rifles. This time a bullet passed through the top of Fargo's hat. A moment later a bullet came so close to Fargo's ear that he could actually hear the projectile singing. It did not sing a merry tune.

And then a final test. Another barbed wire fence approximately a third again as high as the last one. Fargo and his stallion moving so fast now—and the bullets seeming to slip by in ever increasing numbers—that there was no time to prepare for this next jump. Fargo forced thoughts of failure from his mind—the loyal animal shredded by the barbed wire, maybe a leg broken in the fall—and not to mention the possibility of him taking three or four bullets, any one of which could be fatal.

But there was no other choice.

One more barbed wire fence and they'd be free of Manning's land. Fargo had no idea where he'd head next and it didn't matter. His entire mind was concentrated on jumping the fence that lay just ahead. It seemed to grow taller and more insurmountable by the moment.

A blaze of bullets; a hail of shouts, curses; and men with rifles running not far behind him. With so many bullets in the air, maybe he wouldn't have to worry about the jump. Maybe he'd be dead by the time they got to the barbed wire.

And then there it was. And there was no time to think about anything. He clung to the stallion and the stallion responded with a flight of flesh and bone and sheer magnificent equine skill that took both of them gliding across the barbed wire with a few inches to spare.

The gunfire tripled behind him, but Fargo didn't care. He was free of Manning's land and his stallion hadn't been hurt at all. He allowed himself the luxury of feeling pretty damned good for a moment. But only for a moment. With Manning dead and him the prime suspect, there was sure to be even more trouble than before.

8

Ruth Beauregard Tralins had the biggest breasts that had ever passed through town. You would think that a prostitute thus endowed would reap enormous rewards. But Ruth Beauregard Tralins had what you might call a problem. And that was her mouth. Not the size of it nor the shape of it—those were quite fetching, in fact—but rather what came out of that mouth.

In addition to having one of the greatest chests in the West, Ruth Beauregard Tralins also had the meanest temper and the mightiest right hand. And she had opinions. My God, did she have opinions. She felt that she knew everything worth knowing about politics, banking, ranching, religion, sex (naturally enough), fashion, medicine, food, horses, courtship, gambling, and sports—to name but a few of the subjects about which she felt expert. You might be reaching the promised land, her mouth might be full of you, you might be helping her out of her dress—no matter. If you said anything that struck her as disharmonious with the way she ran the universe—wham. She'd crack you upstairs, downstairs, or even right in the furnace if your perceived stupidity irked her.

All of which explained how Ruth Beauregard Tralins was reduced to burglary to supplement her income as a busty lady of the evening.

Tonight, she happened to be in the hotel where Fargo was staying. Most of the people on the floor being of the traveling persuasion, snores pressed early on the silence of the hall where Ruth was setting up her next caper or three. This time of night, rooms got difficult to read. They might sound empty from the hall. But inside could be one of those deceitful bastards who slept without snoring. She'd already had the unfortunate experience of jimmying open a door only to find a non-snorer stretched out on his bed, sound asleep. Luckily, she'd never awakened any of the slumbering men.

Room 212 appeared promising. She'd been listening at the door for four full minutes now. And heard absolutely no sound coming from inside. Worth a try, she decided.

Carefully, she turned the doorknob. Locked. Of course. A buxom woman in a gingham dress, she slid her hand into her pocket and extracted three tiny tools that resembled sticks with hooks on their ends. She proceeded to open the door.

The only light inside came from the dull glow of the street lantern half a block away. Nothing remarkable about the room itself. Standard issue, except maybe a little shabbier than usual.

And best of all—the room was empty.

She set to work.

She found a duffel bag and began going through it. Whoever he was, he wasn't much in the way of things worth stealing. Box of bullets, couple cigars, pouch of cigarette tobacco, soap, razor for shaving, and then clothes. Drifter, she figured. Drifters were worthless to hotel burglars. Usually anything of value they kept on their persons. Likely as not, they didn't have anything of value anyway.

She had just started going through the bureau drawers when she heard the two men sneaking up the hall. She knew they were sneaking because of the way they were whispering. They were up to something.

Then they were at the door. Except they had a key.

Buxom as she was, Ruth Beauregard Tralins was a spry and limber twenty-three years of age. She flung herself to the floor and crawled quickly under the bed—just as the door creaked opened.

They came inside and closed the door behind them.

They still whispered. But now she could make out the words.

"We got to kill Fargo, Heilbronner. We don't have no choice. Manning's dead, and Fargo killed him. If Fargo ever tries to tell anybody that we tried to get him to break into Manning's place and get our money back, people'll think we were a part of it all. And dead or not, Manning's got plenty of friends. Take that chair there, Heilbronner, and sit right in front of the door. Soon as he comes in, you blast him."

"Why don't *you* sit in front of the door and blast him? Why do I have to do it?"

"Because we flipped a coin, remember?"

"Yes, but you wouldn't show me the coin. I'm not sure it had a head and tail. I think it only had a head."

"It was a coin, I tell ya. A plain ordinary, everyday coin, all right? And you lost the flip fair and square, all right? Now you sit down there in that chair and as soon as he opens the door, you blast him, all right? I'll even go drag that chair over here for ya, show you what kind of friend I am."

"You cheated me and you know it, Recard."

"Why don't you talk a little louder so we wake up everybody on the floor, Heilbronner? Boy, you've got a big mouth sometimes. Now here's the chair and you sit down in it and have your gun out and you blast him soon as that door's opened, all right?"

"I still say you cheated me," Heilbronner said. "And cheated me good."

"I've got other things to do," Recard said. "I'll talk to you later."

He left.

Underneath the bed, the lady with the large breasts was working hard to keep from laughing.

Fargo had to risk going back to town. His bankroll was sewn into a secret part of his sheepskin coat. He hadn't needed to touch it for two years. But he sure didn't want to leave it behind.

The problem, of course, was getting in and out of town without being seen. He remembered the steep-sided creek that wound very near town. Good fishing, people said.

His hotel was not much more than a city block from the creek. Getting in the back way shouldn't be much trouble. Reach the hall. Swing open his door. Grab the coat and the rest of his things, race back to the creek where the steep sides would help hide his stallion.

He was halfway to town when he became aware of somebody following behind him at a great distance. . . .

Heilbronner faced the door. Forget Fargo. The man he really wanted to shoot was Recard. Recard had tricked him for sure with a one-headed coin.

Heilbronner started wondering about other things now, too. Like the time his wife and Recard got "stranded" together in a light snowfall they insisted was a blizzard. Or like the time Heilbronner bought a fine stud horse for breeding from Recard—the horse was stolen the very first night it resided in Heilbronner's barn, a friend of his insisting that he'd seen that very same horse being boarded on a train with Recard leading the animal up the ramp himself. Or the times his voluptuous teenage daughter went to visit Recard to teach him how to read and always came back with marks on her neck like somebody had been sucking on it. It was a good thing Heilbronner wasn't a suspicious man because otherwise he would have started wondering about his "friend" now for sure.

Yessir, it was a good thing he wasn't a suspicious man.

Ruth Beauregard Tralins was sick and tired of being under the bed. There was so much dust under there, for one thing, that she was constantly having to stave off a sneeze. For another, her beautiful breasts didn't appreciate being flattened out against the floor this way. Besides, by now she realized who these men were who'd planned Fargo's death. Men who'd been her customers at one time and then signed a petition to rid the town of red light ladies. Ruth Beauregard Tralins did her best to tolerate most kinds of folks. But hypocrites she couldn't abide.

And she didn't care all that much for cold-blooded killers when you came right down to it.. You wanted to kill somebody, at least have the common decency to walk up to him and face him down, give him a chance to defend himself.

But to be lurking in the darkness and shoot a man as soon as he opened the door—

This and their hypocrisy made Recard and Heilbronner two men she despised.

Fargo felt vulnerable in his half-run to the hotel from the creek. Wide open space. Anybody could spot him. Much as Manning had been hated in this town, he'd given the place his own form of law and order. It was funny—scary, sometimes—what people would do for law and order. Put up with any kind of despot who could bring peace, even if it meant killing anybody he decided to or wanted to.

He couldn't see anybody around the back of the hotel. He had his Colt drawn. He wasn't taking any more risks. He wanted his coat, his bankroll, and then he wanted to get the hell out of here.

The hotel grounds smelled of outhouse, seared meat from the café on the first floor, and the garbage waiting to be hauled out to the collective dumping ground.

Inside the hotel, the smells tended to tobacco and whiskey.

He went up the stairs on tiptoe. Gun still drawn.

The second floor hallway was empty. His luck was holding.

Some of the snoring going on was so loud, it should have shimmied the walls. Same with the hawking, the belching, the farting. A symphony of impolite and sometimes irritating noises. None of which the Trails-man, being a true-life legend of the West, ever com-mitted himself, of course.

He found his room, dug his key out, and started to insert it when he heard a man's voice say, "Hey, what the hell?" from the other side of the pine door.

He backed away, raised his right foot, and kicked the door in. He pitched himself to the floor so that if anybody was going to shoot him they'd have to find him first.

And then he got to his feet and laughed out loud.

It was some comical sight, it was, Recard's friend Heilbronner sitting in a chair, unable to move because a large but sumptuously put-together woman had him in a headlock and was squeezing the hell out of him. Heilbronner's face was flushed a lurid red. If she didn't let up soon, Heilbronner was going to die.

When she saw Fargo there in the moonlight, she said, "Say, you were worth saving, after all. I like your looks, mister."

"I don't mind yours, either," Fargo said. He nodded to Heilbronner. She seemed to have forgotten him. But she hadn't relented any on that choke-hold. "Maybe you should ease up on him a little."

"They were going to kill you. They were afraid that because they'd tried to hire you, everybody in town would think they had you kill Manning. And good riddance to Manning, by the way. He was the cheapest bastard in town. He always thought I should give him a discount because he was such an important man. Who the hell ever heard of a discount in my busi-ness?" Then she looked down at Heilbronner's bright-burning face and said, "Oh, I forgot about him."

Heilbronner fell face first out of the chair, slamming his body against the floor.

"I should've let her kill you," Fargo said.

Heilbronner gaped upward. His eyes didn't look fo-cused. His body glistened with sweat. "It was Recard's idea to kill you."

"Is that true?" Fargo asked the woman.

"Nope. They both wanted to kill you. But Recard made him do it."

"He cheated me. He had this one-headed coin." Heilbronner sounded like a whining child.

"Get the hell out of here," Fargo said. "If I ever see you or Recard again, you'll be damn sorry."

Heilbronner was breathless by the time he'd levered his formidable frame upright. "So you really killed Manning?"

"I didn't kill anybody. But somebody sure made it look like I did."

"There'll be a reward out for you. A big one. You better get out of town."

"I was going to till I got up here and found you waiting for me. There isn't anybody in this whole town I trust. So before I leave, I'm going to find out what the hell's really going on. First Li Ping dies and then Huang Chow. And then Manning. There's a connection here somewhere. And since your sheriff won't ever look into it, I'm going to. Now get out of here before I let this very lovely lady finish killing you."

"It was Recard's idea," Heilbronner said as he scrambled toward the door.

When the man was gone, Fargo went to his saddlebags and clothes and checked his sheepskin. The money was still there. "I don't suppose you'd want to tell me what you were doing in my room in the first place?"

"I'm a maid."

"Sure you are. And I'm president of the United States."

She shrugged. "I was going to rob you. Then those two idiots came in." She quickly sketched in her history in town.

He smiled. "Maybe you shouldn't have such strong opinions around your customers."

"I just can't seem to keep my mouth shut." She came over to him, slid her arms around him. "But right now I can think of a way to keep myself occupied. If you're willing, I mean."

One thing a Western legend should never do, Fargo thought, is let himself get distracted from the task at hand—which should have been getting the hell out of this crooked town and never coming back. However, since he had decided to stay and find out what was going on, and clear his name while he was at it, he thought he might as well let himself get *really* distracted with the voluptuous beauty who was pressing herself against him with unmistakable intentions.

Hell, he'd even forgive her for trying to rob him. How could you hold a grudge against somebody who'd just possibly saved your life and was offering herself to you besides?

"Let's see if we can find an empty room," Fargo said. "Because sure as hell McGinley'll come bustin' in here any time now."

Ruth Beauregard Tralins wasn't quite as voluptuous as Faye Manning but she had a pair of hips that were as wise as Socrates. Even before Fargo could make his way from her forehead to her lips she was insinuating herself against him with such seductive force that he was afraid he was going to finish before he started.

Ruth took her time. She was an ear-nibbler, a hickie-planter, a crotch-rubber both before and after he had dropped trou, a massager, an ever-louder gasper, and a hand-guider who took Fargo's fingers to many exotic places, all of which had an explosive effect on her.

She was also something of an athlete. When they finally got down to it, she leapt from the bed and grabbed a chair and then grabbed Fargo and planted him down.

And then she wailed.

The way she went at it, he had the sense that she was competing in a new athletic field event. She was one of the strongest women he'd ever been with, sleek, sure muscles rippling just below silken skin.

She jumped up and down on him with such force, he thought they'd break the chair.

And then she jumped up and yanked him off the chair. She bent over and put her own hands on the chair and presented her backside to him.

He slid his hands up and over her ribs and found her sumptuous breasts, alternately squeezing them and rubbing the nipples with his thumbs. Her juices ran down his legs as he continued searching for the oil gusher he knew was down there somewhere. At one point, he was thrusting so hard, he literally lifted her off the floor with his stiff manhood.

And that was when the chair collapsed. Slam, wham. What had been a respectable piece of furniture was now a pile of kindling. But that didn't slow them down at all. Without ever pulling out, he guided her to the window. She grasped both sides of the frame and he began putting it to her full force again until they collapsed in a spectacular moment of total physical glee and exhaustion.

He rolled them both a cigarette and said, "You want any love talk or anything like that?"

"You any good at it?"

"Not so's you'd notice."

"Then don't worry about it. It's mostly cornball, anyway." She took a deep drag on her cigarette. "That's not what I've been thinkin' about anyway."

"What've you been thinking about?"

"Just wonderin' if his wife had anything to do with it."

"Why his wife?"

"Way he treated her. Used to lock her up for days at a time. Never met a man jealous as he was. Had her followed just about everywhere she went."

"He told you that?"

"Uh-huh. Laughed about it. Said she married him for his money but he outsmarted her. He was going to punish her as long as they lived."

"Why didn't she leave him?"

"Oh. He had an answer to that, too. Said he'd kill her if she ever tried."

"Sounds like a good husband to me."

He got up, got dressed. She did likewise.

She laughed. "I would've cut his privates off and handed them to him. No way I'd take any of that from a man."

It was then the law arrived. They didn't care if they woke people up. There had to be three, maybe four of them clomping down the hall, stopping at Fargo's former room.

"You come out of there, Fargo. Otherwise we're comin' in with four shotguns and takin' care of you on the spot."

Ruth whispered, "You better get out of here. And I mean get out of town—out of the county."

"I'll be sticking around for a while. But leastways I could get myself out of this room, I guess."

The hallway would be suicide. He could jump from this window to a lower roof below.

"You'll have every gun in town looking for you," she said. "I don't care what happens as long as we get to spend a little more time together in the hay. You know how to treat a woman."

He smiled. "Now you going to give me that gold eagle back?"

She feigned indignation. "What gold eagle?"

"The one you scooped off the bureau while you were telling me I knew how to treat a woman."

"Well, Fargo, a lady's got to look out for herself, don't she?" She did a lot of eyelid batting with this line.

He leaned over and kissed her tenderly on the mouth. Then he wrenched her wrist slightly to the left—just enough strength to pry her fingers open—and removed his coin. "Two things I never do, ma'am. Never pay for sex and never believe anything a politician tells me."

He'd managed to spur her into her famous anger.

She threw a roundhouse punch at him that he was able to duck, but barely. He grabbed his belongings and hurried to the window.

"I shoulda made you sweet talk me, Fargo. Served you right."

Then she lunged at him.

He jumped before she could push him.

9

A fancy buggy pulled up in front of a large white frame house on the nicest street in town. The horse pulling the buggy was a sleek bay, every bit as elegant as the vehicle itself. A small glass-encased lantern was mounted on the right side of the buggy, revealing the appealing face and body of Faye Manning who was dressed in a simple white cotton frock, about all the clothing a person could handle on a night like this.

She stepped down from the buggy, tied the reins to a picket of the white fence, opened the gate, and walked briskly up to the front door. She raised the brass knocker in the middle of the door and brought it down hard. Given the silence of the night, she was sure she'd be heard. She wondered idly if she seemed ghostlike, what with the brilliant whiteness of her dress in the moonlight. Shake the old bastard up. A little shaking would be good for him. As the town's leading lawyer—not too hard a trick since the only other attorney was a whiskey-besotted, memory-impaired idler whose incompetence in the courtroom could get you hanged for spitting on the sidewalk—Hiram K. Barnes was way too smug.

Hiram himself answered the door. He was an imposing man and knew it. He'd turned sixty last year but you'd never know it by his erect and muscular frame and the harsh judgment of his ice blue eyes. Only his white hair gave away his age. And the hair was beautiful—sleek and dramatic on a head already sleek and dramatic. He wore trousers and a white shirt he hadn't tucked in.

"I was expecting you, Faye." The smile quickly turned to a smirk. "I was sure that after you'd mourned your husband for a few minutes, you'd head right over here to see how the will read."

"Let's go to your office so we can see."

The smirk again. "Come in. I'm way ahead of you. As soon as I heard that Del was dead, I went to the office and took the will from my safe and brought it back here."

"You never did have any faith in me, Hiram. And I was such a good wife."

He laughed, throwing his regal head back as he did so. "A tart with a sense of humor. If I didn't worry about disease, I would have bedded you a long time ago."

"Oh, no, Hiram. I have strict rules about who I sleep with. Rule number one is to never sleep with a corpse."

For just one wonderful exhilarating moment she saw the pain her remark had put in his eyes. But he quickly composed himself, stood aside, and offered her a mock bow as he waved her inside.

She had always dreaded coming here. The huge furniture coupled with the dark walls and drapes gave the place the ambience of a mausoleum or mortuary. The British seascapes, so carefully framed and adroitly hung, did break up the tedious darkness somewhat— but not enough.

He led her through the house to a small den off the main hall. The den was as gloomy as the rest of the house. Dark leather furnishings, more brooding curtains and walls, and a desk that must have weighed five hundred pounds. He pointed to a deep chair and proceeded to pour each of them a snifter of brandy. "Del loved this brandy."

"Good for him," she said.

He stared at her a long moment. "You're almost as ruthless as I am, Faye." He didn't smile when he said it.

"He used to beat me, Hiram. One night he even threw me down the stairs after he thought I'd flirted with one of the ranch hands.

He seated himself. And smirked again. "The helpless woman role doesn't really suit you. In fact, if Fargo hadn't killed Del, I would've thought you'd done it. He was a very jealous man, that's true. But you gave him a lot of reason to be jealous. And you berated him for his prowess in bed."

"His lack of prowess," she laughed. "That's the way you should say it. He'd satisfy himself in a minute or two and then hop off and disappear somewhere in the house."

"I thought it was only whores who needed to be sated by sex," he said, quite stuffily. "My understanding has always been that good women don't really like sex. They just endure it."

"Oh? Well, you should hear some of those 'good women' talk when there aren't any men around. You'd be surprised what they like and don't like."

"If they talk the way you imply they do, they're not good women."

"If you say so, Hiram." She pointed to the papers on his desk. "Now let's get to work, shall we?"

They broke into Fargo's room, men with shotguns and a hunger for killing. They hadn't gotten to hang Huang Chow, they'd stomped but not killed Fargo, and now when they were sure they had him cornered, he wasn't there. A pretty frustrating situation.

The three deputies left the room. McGinley stayed to check things over one more time. Two of the deputies were going home, all the fire gone now that Fargo had outsmarted them again. One deputy was headed back to the office where he planned to stoke up on coffee and look around town in case Fargo hadn't cleared out.

Down the hall, Ruth Beauregard Tralins waited until the law had cleared out before she ventured into the hallway. She'd already been warned to stay out of hotels. If she was going to whore, she had to whore out on the edge of town like everybody else. And if she was going to steal from hotel rooms—well, women could go to jail, too.

She waited.

Nobody had ever accused this crew of being light-footed. They sounded like a stampede of drunken stumbling steers going down the hall and then down the stairs.

At last she could open the door, go back to her little room and get some sleep. She went out into the hall, and there, standing in front of Fargo's old room and staring right at her, was none other than the newly appointed Sheriff McGinley. He didn't have any fondness for her. She'd always made him pay full price and once he asked her to do something so vile she threatened to tell everybody in town if he didn't walk right out her door and never come back. Ever since, he'd get all embarrassed and nervous whenever they'd pass each other on the street. He was afraid of her, afraid she might tell, though as a prostitute of honor, she never would unless he tried to hurt her.

"Well, well," he said, and she knew immediately that he was drinking because he sounded so sure of himself, as if the liquor had waterlogged his memory. "Lookit here."

"Leave me alone, McGinley."

He came up to her, jangle of spurs, scent of sweat, lump of cheek tobacco. He seemed about to say something but then he stopped—stood absolutely still—and then bent like a bird to sniff her, his nose making a low whistling sound when he did.

"Who's your victim tonight?"

"None of your damned business."

"You better not take that tone with me, Ruth. I'm the high sheriff now."

"The high sheriff? What a stupid title."

"You don't get smart. Now I'm askin' you nice, what you been up to tonight?"

"I ain't been stealin'."

"That just means you couldn't find nothin' worth stealin'. And anyway, stealin' ain't what I want to know about."

Her eyes narrowed as she began to understand why he'd sniffed her and then walked back to Fargo's room.

"You got a real strange perfume on, Ruth."

"Most men like it. Real men, anyway."

He grabbed her arm with such force that she swore his fingers penetrated all the way to the bone. "You were in Fargo's room earlier tonight, weren't you? And now you're gonna tell me everything." His fingers ground even deeper into her arm. "Ain't I right, Ruth? Ain't you gonna tell me every single thing you two talked about?"

When Hiram told her who the chief beneficiary was, Faye sat back and said, "I wish my folks were here to hear this."

Hiram Barnes did a double take when she spoke. He had never heard Faye sound this melancholy. It had to be a false sentiment. This was one of the most ruthless women he'd ever known.

"You don't know what they went through. They never had anything, Hiram. My mother died before she was twenty-five. The doctor said that she'd just worn out. My papa died before he was thirty. Same thing. Worn out—between keeping the farm going and raising us four kids. He loved my mother so much he wouldn't even consider getting married again. He was a true blue man, my father. You don't find many men like him around anymore."

Hiram was almost caught up in her speech when she became the Faye he was more familiar with. "How much is in cash and how much in property?"

"I'd have to work up those figures. Like all wealthy men, his wealth went up and down."

"I want to know by noon tomorrow."

Hiram raised a skeptical eyebrow. "I'm not a young man, as you so ungallantly pointed out, Faye. I need my sleep. To have those figures for you, I'd have to go to the office right now and start work."

"Then do it."

She was enjoying herself. Now that she was named beneficiary of the will, she was, in effect, Hiram's boss. And she meant to make him damned aware of that fact. She wouldn't abide his smirks, his insinuations, his insults any longer. The estate could earn him a lot of money in administrative fees and they both knew it. And to keep on getting those fees, he was, for the first time in their relationship, going to have to cater to her. She was the beautiful princess and he was the unimportant knave.

"And when I come into town to get the figures, I'll also have a list of all the people I want fired out at the ranch."

He couldn't resist. "Would any of those be men you've slept with?"

She smiled at his pettiness. "You're just jealous, Hiram. You should see yourself when I come around. There's nothing more disgusting than some old man wanting a young woman. And while we're at it—let's make it eleven instead of noon."

"But that's impossible. I need more time to—"

"Eleven," she said and stood up. "Or I'll wire San Francisco and get another attorney."

She swept to the door, lady of the manor. "And the next time you make any remarks about my virtue, Hiram, I'm going to tell your wife about that little Mexican girl you keep visiting every week."

Fargo spent the night in his bedroll on the edge of town. He was a light sleeper and kept his Colt on his chest for easy access.

Before finally falling asleep, he took the time to work his way back through everything that had happened since meeting Lala Huang. Her brother allegedly kills his friend in Manning's den. He is in turn almost lynched. Later on Manning kills him in cold blood. Before he died, Huang Chow told his sister that he had come into money—this after he and his friend went away for a week. But where? And where did they get money? And where was the money? He sensed a mysterious connection among the three men and their deaths. Manning had seemed determined to kill Huang Chow no matter what. But why? Did Huang Chow have something on Manning?

And who killed Manning? He considered his suspects. Manning's wife was chief among them—he assumed she stood to come into real money. Lala Huang, bitter about Huang Chow's cold-blooded death, was also a suspect. Manning had a lawyer who knew all about Manning's affairs. Could the lawyer have done it? And what about Recard and Heilbronner? They certainly had reason enough to kill Manning.

There was a good chance that Manning had killed both Huang Chow and Li Ping, but why? And then why in turn had Manning been killed? And what connected all these deaths?

Exhausted, he fell asleep.

10

He touched the Colt upon his chest even before his eyes came open.

Brush crackling. No matter how gently a person tried to walk on ground like this, there was always a twig, a crusty patch, even a wilted flower that transmitted the softest step.

It was near dawn and chilly with the half-moon still vivid in the starry sky. Fargo lay on a flat section of grass and waited.

His uninvited guest was now behind the oak tree to his right. Fargo had one eye half open. When the intruder came a couple of steps closer—

Sandra carried her six-shooter in front of her as she made her way around the oak and started to close on the few feet separating her from Fargo. She wanted his saddlebags. They lay next to him. She felt she could get them without disturbing him.

But she was disabused of this notion with such violent surprise that when Fargo suddenly jumped to his feet, pivoted, and shot the gun out of her hand, she lost the cool and poise she prided herself on. Something dangerously close to a scream choked in her throat. It did not escape her mouth but she knew it was there and that was enough. Her pride had been hurt far more than her bullet-grazed gun hand.

He was in complete control—even smiling at her— and she despised him for it.

"I knew you'd make your move sooner or later."

"I should have shot you in your sleep."

"I'm just as glad you didn't. Now who the hell are you and why are you following me?"

"You knew I was following you?"

"Lady, I learned tracking from Indian scouts. I picked up your scent when you followed me from town the night I went to Manning's place."

"Then why didn't you do something?"

His smile was even more irritating now. "You didn't seem to be any particular danger. I figured anybody who couldn't track a person better than you probably wasn't much of a threat."

"You're an insolent bastard, Fargo."

The contempt in her voice told him a few things about her. She came from a moneyed, probably educated background. She had the superiority that comes out whenever anybody of her class talks to somebody they feel is of a lower class. And she clearly thought that Fargo was of a pretty low order.

Her riding costume—and that's what it was, the dark blouse real silk, the riding trousers sewn to fit her slender but consummately erotic body perfectly—was also revealing of more than her upthrust breasts and the gentle slopes of her hips. It also said money, breeding, status. Why the hell was somebody like her following him around? If she had some secret reason to dislike him and want him dealt with, why didn't she hire a gunny to do the job for her?

When she started to bend down to retrieve the weapon he'd shot away, he said, "I'll tell you when you can have your gun back."

She froze, half-bent over. "Who the hell do you think you are?"

"I know who I am—the man you tried to kill a few minutes ago."

"To kill?" Her laugh was as rich with scorn as her words. "You wouldn't be worth killing, Fargo. I simply wanted to look in your saddlebag."

"For what?"

"For none of your damned business, that's what."

He beckoned to his saddlebags with his gun. "Go ahead and look."

"What?"

"Go look in my saddlebags. I want to see what was worth risking your life to get. Since you won't tell me, I mean."

"So you can shoot me in the back while I'm searching them?"

Fargo shook his head. "Lady, if I wanted to kill you, I would've shot you the second I drew down on you. I just want to know what the hell you're so damned curious about."

"You mean it? You'll really let me look?"

"Be my guest."

From the way she inched over to his saddlebags, constantly glancing over her shoulder as if he was about to fire his Colt, he could see that she really did believe he might kill her. He was half-tempted to fire at her feet, scare some of that arrogance out of her.

She spent a good five minutes with the saddlebags. She'd take something out, hold it up to the dawning light to examine it, put it back, and then take something else out for inspection. The most exciting thing she came across was his new comb which she examined with the scrutiny of a doc looking at a strange mole on somebody's arm. How long could you look over a comb?

She finally gave up, walked back to him. "That everything you own, Fargo?"

"Just about."

"You've got a pretty pathetic life."

"Well, thank you. That's nice of you to point out."

"Maybe I've been following you for nothing."

"Now that'd be a shame, wouldn't it? A princess like you wasting her valuable time?"

She was close enough to slap him and did just that. She did it with an open hand, too, catching him right between nose and jawline on the right side of his face. Hard enough to make his eyes water.

"They killed my brother, you sonofabitch. This isn't anything to make fun of."

"What the hell are you talking about? Who's your brother?" he said. He wouldn't mind slapping her right back but he'd given up stomping kittens and setting nuns on fire for Lent. He supposed he shouldn't be slapping princesses around, either.

She surprised him by breaking into tears with such violence that she collapsed straight down to the ground where she went into spasms of grief that were almost frightening to see.

Her name, she said, was Sandra Evans, of the Sacramento Evanses. She said "of the Sacramento Evanses" with a certain haughtiness. He probably would have been impressed if he'd known more about California high society.

Her story was almost Biblical in its simplicity. Her younger brother, David, took to whiskey and women at an early age. Her father had to use all of his influence—and a good deal of his money—to keep David out of prison. Over his young years, he'd gone from boozy pranks to boozy felonies. He'd even shot a man once. Luckily for both of them, the man lived. Thanks to the family's largesse his target refused to press charges, claiming he couldn't remember what his assailant had looked like. Their father had a stroke and everybody in the family blamed David for it. David had broken the old man's heart so many times that the patriarch had lost the will to live.

Then David did something nobody had expected him to. Or even *believed* he could do. He quit drinking. As he later told his sister, he had a terrible nightmare about visiting his father's grave on a windy, rain-swept night. He knew that he had put his father in the ground—all his years of drinking and womanizing and gambling and fighting—the old man had simply given in to death. In the nightmare, he started calling out the old man's name, promising his father that he would change his ways. And damned if it didn't work—at least in the curious logic of nightmares—and the father rose from the grave and took his son in his arms and returned to full and exuberant life.

David took this nightmare as a sign. He not only quit drinking, he took a job. His father wanted him to work in the family mining business, some kind of executive position. But David liked being outdoors; he also liked a frequent change of scenery. So David took the lowly position of shotgun guard on gold shipments for his father's company. It wasn't a prestigious position, the old man confided in Sandra, but it sure beat hanging around a saloon all day and getting into trouble.

Six weeks into his new job, two men in masks stuck up the wagon he was guarding, a massive shipment of gold aboard. David was killed because he wouldn't throw down his gun.

"The other guard had the impression that both of the robbers were Chinese," Sandra said.

The guard managed to stay calm. He noticed that one of the robber's horses had a limp. When he got to town, he went straight to the livery and asked if anybody'd brought a horse in with a limp. The livery-man said yes, two Chinese immigrants. He said he got the impression they came from some huge ranch to the east because he saw the brand had two large merged Ms on it.

"My father died two days after he heard of David's death. I hired a detective to find the two Chinese and this big ranch. He wired me that he thought he'd found it and that he'd send me a full report soon. I never heard from him again. A couple of weeks later he was found at the bottom of a ravine. The animals hadn't left much of him. The local sheriff went through the detective's things but didn't find any report. Neither did the Sacramento office the man worked out of.

"That's when I took over myself. It was the right thing to do, anyway. My brother was dead and so was my father."

Fargo said, "That merged double M—Manning?"

She nodded. "Manning."

"You think he was behind the robbery?"

"Of course."

"You sure they weren't acting on their own? Manning was the richest man in this section of the State."

She shook her head. "As of a year ago he was. But he had a lot of businesses go bad on him in the last ten, eleven months. I checked into his finances. Everything was mortgaged. They were even going to foreclose on his shipping business. He needed money desperately. The gold enabled him to pay off his debts."

"Were you the one who hid in his den and knocked me out and then killed him?"

Her voice was bitter against the birdsong and yellow sky of dawning. "I wish I had been. I wanted that satisfaction. But I didn't get it. Somebody else did."

"So now your work's done?"

"You mean because Manning's dead?"

"Right."

"Hardly, Fargo. That gold he took belonged to my father. Since I can't have the satisfaction of killing him, I want the satisfaction of getting what's left of the gold."

"There's some left?"

"A lot left," Sandra said. "I had our family accountant find out how much his total debt was and compared that to how much gold he got. There should be a quarter of a million dollars left. That's why Manning killed Huang Chow and Li Ping. I'm sure he promised them a big share of it. But he killed Li Ping and blamed it on Huang Chow and then he took the first chance he got to kill Huang Chow."

"But why wouldn't Huang Chow have told the law what was going on?"

"Think about it, Fargo. Manning had those two just where he wanted them. If Huang Chow or Li Ping went to the law, they'd have to confess that they'd killed my brother—a white man. You know how long it would be before a lynch mob dragged them from their cells? Chinamen don't go around killing white men and live very long afterward."

She was smart, Fargo saw. And bitter. He had no doubt that she really would've killed Manning, along with Huang Chow and Li Ping if she'd had the chance.

"So how do you go about finding the gold?"

"I figure Manning's killer must know where it is. Once I find him. I'll find the gold."

"You could get killed yourself."

"Right now I don't much give a damn about that. My brother and father are dead. That's all I care about." She set her low-brimmed hat back on her elegant head. "I assume you've stuck around here to clear your name."

"I don't want to have a murder charge hanging over me. I like to roam and that could present a hell of a problem."

"Then join me. We both want the same thing—whoever killed Manning."

Fargo thought about it for a time, rolling a cigarette as he did so. "There's one problem."

"What's that?"

"I can't go into town and talk to people. Everybody'd recognize me."

"Not after I get done with you."

"Meaning what?"

"Meaning that I've spent a lot of time doing what the local newspaper calls 'amateur theatricals.' I learned a whole lot of things about disguising myself. And I could do the same for you."

"Well, I'll be damned," Fargo said.

For the first time, a laugh came from that erotic, if dour, mouth of hers. "I imagine we both will be, Fargo."

"You still think they'll recognize you?"

Six hours later, after going into town and buying a

large carpetbag full of various items, Sandra Evans returned to the campsite and began working on creating a disguise for Fargo.

By the time she was done, he stood before her as a Mexican with a serape and a large sombrero. He wore squinty little eyeglasses and had a deep red scar angled across his jaw. He also wore loose, faded work clothes. No gun, no knife scabbard. She took a mirror the size of a book and held it in front of him.

"I'll be damned."

"I think you said that before, Fargo. Anybody who looks close'll see what we're up to. But the trick is to sneak you in and out without anybody having *time* to look close."

"I want to see Manning's widow."

"Makes sense. She has the most to gain."

"She goes to town most mornings. We can stop her on the way in."

"She doesn't take any guards with her, all the enemies her husband had?"

"She's under the impression she's tough."

"How about me, Fargo? Am I tough?" There was a gentle sexuality in the brown eyes he'd never seen before. A bit of friendly amusement.

"I don't know about tough but you're sure smart."

"Well, thank you, Fargo."

"And you're sure pretty, too. Beautiful, in fact."

"Why, Fargo, two compliments inside of a minute? I'm impressed."

"You could always call me something besides 'Fargo.' "

"You like 'Shithead?' "

He laughed. "Maybe you *are* tough, after all."

"You think of anybody we can pay a visit to tonight?"

"Yeah. Manning had a lawyer."

"Hiram Barnes. He wouldn't tell me anything."

"Maybe he'll change his mind. The way I get it," Fargo said, "he knew everything there was to know about Manning."

"Why don't I fix us something to eat and by then it'll be dark. We'll go into town."

"All we've got is jerky."

"I picked up a few things, Fargo. I sure as hell wasn't going to eat jerky. My God, remember, I'm a spoiled rich girl. And I plan to keep acting like one."

Yeah, Fargo decided, in her complicated way, she was not only smart but tough—if constantly getting your way was a definition of tough.

11

Esmerelda said, "You're nervous tonight."

"I did all right, didn't I?"

She smiled. She knew all about male pride. "You did fine. Like always, Hiram."

Hiram Barnes still brooded about Faye Manning's caustic remark about him being "a corpse." She should give him a try sometime. She'd see how dead his sexual drive was. White hair be damned.

Esmerelda Arenas lay next to him in the double bed he'd bought for them. She was a thirty-six-year-old woman whose husband and two boys were off in the gold country somewhere. The Golden Mountain, the Chinese called this State. How foolish that was. So many men had trekked west—the so-called forty-niners—only to die broken and bitter in some creek somewhere. She decided that to be the kept woman of a wealthy lawyer was not so bad. She had kept her shape and her quite pretty face. The others in the small village on the edge of the white man's town knew of this liaison. Most of them said nothing. Life was so hard, they could sympathize, her with no men and no way to earn a living but to become a gringo's servant.

Her two-room abode—he couldn't bring himself to call it a "house," that would be a perversion of the word—was spotless as always, the walls vibrant with colorful decorative blankets, the sparse furnishings in the attractive Spanish style.

"Do you ever dream of me?" Esmerelda said, laying a naked arm gently across his chest.

"Oh, don't start this again."

"You could lie. Flatter me."

"You're too sensible to lie to, Esmerelda. You're the most sensible woman I've ever known."

"Do you lie to your wife—other than about me?"

"All the time."

"She is not sensible."

He smiled. "She's a very foolish woman. She never quits reminding me that she grew up on some damned fancy street in Philadelphia and that she sacrificed her entire social life to come west with me."

"She must have loved you very much."

"She was three months pregnant when we got married."

Esmerelda giggled. "What did the people on her fancy street say about that?"

"They didn't know. We headed west right after the wedding. The only outward sign was that she threw up every morning but nobody on the street knew anything about it. Her folks sure wouldn't tell anybody. They wanted to kill both of us. Her father's father had hanged a couple of women he accused of being witches. He was a judge in Rhode Island. That's the kind of people she came from. So you can imagine what they thought of her being pregnant before she got married."

He clutched a hand to his forehead then and groaned.

"The headache again?"

"Yes."

"Would whiskey help?"

"It's Manning being killed. I can't relax. I don't know what's going to happen now. If Faye gets an accountant in there—"

She massaged his shoulders and then his neck. "What if she does get an accountant? How will that hurt you?"

He couldn't believe he was about to tell somebody

about it. But Esmerelda was the only person in the world he trusted. Certainly not his wife or his two pretentious, selfish daughters. Just this woman who was his whore. "I had to borrow money from time to time."

She stopped massaging. "That isn't what you really mean to say, is it?"

He sighed. "No I guess not. I took money from Manning's account without telling him. Spent it on some investments I'd made that went bad. And—"

"And the money was never returned."

"No, it was never returned."

She laughed lustily and began massaging his neck again. "So the next time you become angry with me and call me a cheap wetback slut, I can call you a filthy gringo thief?"

He had to smile. She was cunning and clever. He sure had to give her that. "Yes, you have my permission to call me that."

"Now I have a weapon."

He reached up on his shoulder and took her hand. "You've had a weapon all along, my sweet. A hell of a lot more powerful weapon than any man will ever have. And I must say that I appreciate the way you take care of it—always so sweet and clean and ready for me."

"That is a nice thought, Hiram. That I have a weapon so powerful."

"It's the truth."

She giggled and kissed his shoulder. "Yes, I know it's true. But I hate to boast. I want you to think of me as shy and modest."

She was about halfway through this last remark when the front door opened—they were in the second room and could not see from here. The sound of boots and spurs came loud and dangerous on the silence.

Fargo, not being a dunce, figured out that two people in a bedroom were probably doing something more intimate than darning socks. He stood in the middle of the large front room and said, "Get your clothes on, Barnes, and get out here."

"Who're you?" Barnes asked from the bedroom.

"Somebody who's going to come in there and drag you out by your short and curlies if you don't get a move on."

Fargo could hear them whispering to each other. Hopefully, Barnes wouldn't be foolish enough to try and shoot it out.

"Just a minute," Barnes said.

Squeak of bed, rustle of clothes, more whispers.

He came out with hands up, a mature man but a striking one. He hadn't buttoned his dress shirt, though he had fastened his suspenders. His trousers were gray. His feet were gray. He didn't look scared. He looked irritated. He was obviously a man who had great control over his life and he didn't like anybody who took that control from him.

"I don't have much money on me," he said.

Just then the woman appeared in the bedroom doorway. She had a regal face and imposing body. She was dressed in a dark robe that gave her skin an even more burnished look. She was a real beauty and her eyes suggested both intelligence and a certain patience and wisdom.

"He wouldn't be here for money, Hiram," she said gently, as if speaking to a child. There was great warmth in her voice; and even more warmth in the way she slid her arm through Barnes's. This happened sometimes, though it was rare—a man finding in a mistress not only the sex, but the fondness and tenderness he couldn't find at home.

"Then what would he be here for?" Hiram said, sounding confused. "He comes in here and—"

"I want to talk to you about Del Manning," Fargo said. He tried to fake a Mexican accent.

Esmerelda laughed. "That's very bad acting," she said, obviously unable to get a good look at Fargo's face, which was hidden by the vast sweep of the sombrero brim.

"I agree," Sandra Evans said as she came through the door.

"Maybe I could try a Hungarian accent," Fargo said. "I think I'd be better at that."

Esmerelda laughed out loud. Barnes snapped, "What the hell's going on here?"

"We were listening at the window," Fargo said. "So you embezzled from Manning. Maybe he found out about it and you got scared and killed him."

"Why don't you take off that stupid sombrero so I can get a look at you?" Barnes said.

"You didn't answer his question," Sandra said. "You had a good reason to kill Manning. If he told everybody what you'd done, you'd be ruined in this community. You might even do some jail time."

He aged five years just standing there, Barnes did. He looked with great, solemn sadness down at the woman he loved and shook his head. "That would be a good reason to murder him," he said, glancing up at Fargo. "But I wasn't there. I was here and Es will vouch for me."

"He was here. And worried. Until tonight I wasn't sure why."

. "Until tonight? Why tonight?" Fargo said.

"Because tonight he told me the truth. What you heard at the window." Esmerelda shook her head. She seemed as solemn and sad as Barnes now. She'd made a joke of it earlier—about how she could now call him a thief when he called her a slut—but the humor was gone. All that remained was the husk of a once-imperious attorney who'd given in to the shabbiest of all lawyerly deceits—stealing from his clients.

"Did you know anything about a deal he made with Huang Chow and Li Ping?" Fargo asked.

"Not a thing, why? What sort of deal would he make with his servants?" Barnes said. "He didn't hold Chinamen in very high regard. I can't imagine him making any kind of deal with them."

Fargo believed him. Barnes's concern was clearly

his guilt and fear over his embezzlement. He could still be destroyed. Easily. An accountant could find the discrepancy, begin to whisper about it to various townspeople—there wouldn't even have to be any formal charges. Gossip alone could destroy his reputation.

Fargo said, "Was there any special place Manning ever went when he was worried about something?"

Barnes shrugged. "Not that I know of. For one thing, if he was worried about anything, he generally found somebody to take it out on—his wife or me or one of his employees. He liked to spread the misery around."

Esmerelda slid her arm around Barnes's waist. "Hiram would be so angry when he came here. After a session like that with Manning, I mean. Angry—and then despondent."

"I'd put myself in the place where Manning was about fifty percent of my income. I never should have let any one person have that kind of control over me."

Fargo said, "Did he have a cabin anywhere?"

"No," Barnes said.

"A boat of any kind?"

"Afraid not." Then: "What're you looking for, anyway?"

"It doesn't matter," Fargo told the lawyer.

As soon as he'd spoken, he saw Esmerelda's face brighten. "Wait, Hiram. What about the graveyard?"

"Everybody goes to the graveyard," Hiram said. "That isn't anything special."

"The way he went to it, it was," she said. "Once, even twice a week."

"What about the graveyard?" Fargo said.

Esmerelda smiled at him. "You're disappointing me, you know. Not only can't I see your face, I miss your Mexican accent."

Fargo liked her. He suspected she was all the things Barnes's wife wasn't. He even felt a tug of sympathy for Barnes. It would be difficult to walk away from the proper life he'd so carefully built for himself, and then start a new life with his mistress. But maybe things would change now. Powerful forces were at play in the lawyer's life. Manning was dead. And Barnes's most desperate client was now himself—embezzlement had made him a criminal.

"Maybe some other time I'll go back to the accent," Fargo said wryly. "For now I want to hear more about this graveyard."

"His youngest sister," Barnes began. "Only person I ever knew Manning to really love. Doted on her. She was a very pretty girl but really shy and awkward around people."

"What happened to her?"

"Got thrown from a horse he'd bought her when she turned eighteen. Their folks had died when a riverboat sank a few years earlier. He'd raised her since that time. I think he always blamed himself for buying her that horse. When he was drunk, he'd always say that she'd still be alive it wasn't for him. He killed the horse himself. And from the way he told it, it wasn't a clean kill, either. He beat it to death with a two-by-four."

"Where's this graveyard?"

Barnes told him.

Fargo glanced at Sandra Evans. She nodded almost imperceptibly.

"I appreciate your time," Fargo said.

"That's it? You just leave now?" Barnes said.

"Yes," Fargo said. "Unless you'd like me to shoot you—or maybe try out my accent again."

"Oh, please, just a couple of sentences. It was so bad." Esmerelda looked like a sweet child pleading for her uncle to give her another piece of candy. "I'll treasure it forever."

Fargo smiled at her sarcasm and then moved on.

"I'll bet my blanket is a lot warmer and softer than yours," Fargo said.

"You don't know anything about my blanket," Sandra Evans said.

"No, but I know an awful lot about mine."

She made an amused sound that wasn't quite a laugh. "If I ask you something, will you tell me the truth?"

"To the best of my ability."

They were in a barn. While sleeping on hard, cold ground with all kinds of curious, smelly, and occasionally diseased animals was a lot of fun, Fargo had decided, just for the hell of it, to upgrade his sleeping arrangements. They found a ranch with a barn a pretty good distance from the house, tied up their horses behind a copse of pine trees, and carried their bedrolls into the large red structure. The place smelled of oil, road apples, hay, leather, wood, grain, and the dirt floor.

"Fargo, listen to me."

"All right."

"It's eighty degrees."

"Uh-huh."

"So why do I care if I have a warm blanket?"

"Because it gets cold in the middle of the night."

"First of all, Fargo, it almost *is* the middle of the night and it's hotter than hell."

"I guess that's a good point."

"And second of all, you didn't answer my question."

"I didn't answer it because you didn't ask it."

"I didn't ask it because I knew you wouldn't answer it."

"Try me."

She had been spreading her bedroll out on a narrow stall filled with a large golden swell of fine-smelling hay. She stopped. "All right. When was the last time you slept with a woman?"

"Months ago."

"Uh-huh. See my point? That's why I didn't ask you. Because I knew you'd lie."

"All right. Weeks ago."

"Just shut up, Fargo."

"Not that *many* weeks ago, I'll admit. But *several* weeks ago."

She went back to making out her bed. She didn't say anything.

"Well, maybe not several." He leaned against the edge of the stall and watched her. She had a fine bottom and those little wrists he liked on a lady. "You're not listening, are you?"

"No, I certainly am not."

"Why?"

She kept right on making her bed. "Because you had a chance to tell me the truth and you lied every time."

"What's so important about it anyway?"

She stood up, her back still to him, appraised her work with her hands on her hips. "Because, Fargo, I'd like to think that if we *did* do something it would have some meaning in that dim cowboy mind of yours."

"I'm not a cowboy. I'm a drifter."

"Ah. Now that's something to be proud of. A drifter."

"And if we did do something, I'd be right pleased to be with you. You're a fine woman. You're smart and you've got a sense of humor."

She finally turned and faced him. "Well, Fargo, I have to say, I'm impressed. That sounded like an honest compliment."

"It was. And you've also got a right nice bottom."

" 'A right nice bottom,' " she mocked. "You must spend all your spare time writing poetry."

He grinned, knowing exactly where this was going. He played the hayseed even more, having fun with it. "That's me. Writin' that poetry every chance I get."

Without any warning or ceremony, she began unbuttoning her blouse, every molecule of which he had memorized many times over. "C'mere you big stupid drifter."

"My pleasure."

He took two steps forward and she slid her hand over his crotch. "Well, well," she said, rubbing his enormous instrument. "Look what I found." She wanted this one to be quick. She dropped to her knees, freed his steed, and began to stroke it as if it were a treasure she'd been seeking for many long years. When she had driven him to a kind of mindless, gasping need, she stood up and walked a few feet away.

She stood there and stripped, not making any special fuss about disrobing. But then she didn't have to. The sight of her perfect, uptilted breasts, and then the lovely thatch of pubic hair riding atop the glory of her wet dark sex was far more erotic than any striptease could ever be.

She lay in the grass, spreading her legs to make his entrance easy and simple, her hands fixed now on his buttocks so she could grind his shaft as deep and hard as possible inside her.

The sounds of pure, sheer animal pleasures sang out from their coupling as he went ever deeper.

And when they were done, he wiped himself off on the long grass and then allowed himself to fall down next to her.

"Thanks," she said, as they got dressed.

"Thank *you*."

"I think I needed that more than you did."

"How come?"

"Because for me it *has* been a long time. I was engaged and everything was fine. But then my brother and father died and he didn't like the way I changed. He said I scared him and that I was obsessed and that I was going to get myself killed. He broke off our engagement as soon as I told him I was headed out here."

"Well, I'll be happy to keep an eye on you."

"Yeah, I'll bet you will." She snuggled up against him.

Fargo had been getting groggy so when the voice came it sounded almost supernatural. There was Fargo and there was Sandra Evans—but who the hell was the other woman? And even more, exactly where the hell was she hiding and how long had she been there?

She had been in the loft up and across from them, with a clear view of their lovemaking every time she chose to sneak a peek around a bale of hay.

Then she'd snuck down a ladder near the far end of the barn and tiptoed up to surprise them. Hard to tell which was more menacing—her shotgun or her face. Fargo decided her face. She had some kind of skin disease that gave her cheeks a red scaly surface like a lizard. She had one blind white eye, no teeth, and white hair so filthy it looked black in places. Her gingham dress had been patched so many times it was hard to tell where the original material started and ended. She was so filthy her odor trumped that of even all the horseshit. The barn wasn't any better taken care of than she was.

She said, "Ain't seen a big one like that in a long time, mister."

"You have a good time watching us, did you?" Fargo said.

"Wish the gal had a little more meat on her was all." Her words were mushy sounding. Teeth would have improved their clarity.

Then she shouted.

Fargo wasn't sure *what* she shouted but he guessed it was a name of some kind. She then said, "He'll want to kill you."

"Who will?" Fargo said, as Sandra slid her arms through his and held on tight. He was surprised she would show this much dependence on a man. She must have just now realized—as Fargo had the moment this crone appeared, that they were in the presence of a madwoman.

"My boy, Lester."

"Good old Lester. Is he as crazy as you are?"

She surprised him by cackling out a laugh. "Oh, he's a *lot* crazier than I am. Lester talks to dead people."

"He probably gets lonely."

And then Lester was there. He was sort of disappointing. Fargo had been expecting a strapping shirtless and shoeless monster in bib overalls chewing on a dead possum with one hand while he scratched his butt with the other. And he'd be drooling a lot and kind of muttering to himself. Maybe having one of those conversations with dead people his ma had mentioned.

Lester was maybe five-foot-three, bald, with the same kind of facial skin disease his mom wore. He carried a shotgun and wore a dress much like his mother's, with all the patching and things. He spoke in a voice so deep that he practically rattled the rafters.

"You see her naked, Ma?"

"I sure did."

"She purty?"

"Real purty. But kinda skinny."

"She sure has a purty face."

Fargo must have looked surprised.

Ma said, "Jes' cause he wears my dresses don't mean he don't have an eye for the ladies, mister."

"That's good to know, Ma," Fargo said. "Makes me feel a whole lot better."

"Say, what's your name, mister?"

"Why?"

"Because there's a re-ward out for a man named Fargo. And we could sure use that re-ward." She squinted at him. "You're probably him."

"I hate to disappoint you, Ma, but my name's Blade, Alex Blade."

"Who's got a name like Alex Blade?" she snapped. "That sounds made up. Don't that sound made up, Lester?"

"Sure does sound made up, Ma." Lester was in the process of raping Sandra with his eyes. Fargo was pretty sure that Sandra found Lester attractive. What woman wouldn't? Any man with a stomach-turning facial rash who totes a shotgun, talks to the dead, and wears a size two dress was husband material for sure.

Ma said, "I'm a-ridin' into town and fetchin' the law, and puttin' you in charge of these two. And there'll be hell to pay if you let 'em go."

"You don't worry about that none, Ma. I'll kill 'em before I let 'em go."

"Well, if you have to kill 'em, don't cut 'em up and cook 'em before I get back. We needs to show the law that they was actually here. Plus we don't want to start no rumors about ourselves in town. The kinda meals we like is nobody else's business. You keep a eye on 'em," Ma said.

"You bet I will, Ma," Lester said, scratching the rash on his face.

The newly appointed Sheriff McGinley spent the early part of the morning taking advantage of his shiny fine badge. Sheriff Duncan had always managed to buy himself new clothes and new boots and even cigars and whiskeys at great discounts. McGinley decided to give it a try himself. Though he cadged a new suit, a nice pair of Texas boots, and a cheap feel from the woman who helped run the general store, he'd had to practically threaten folks to get their largesse.

That wasn't the only matter on McGinley's mind this morning, of course. Like just about everybody else in town, he was trying to figure out what would happen now that Del Manning was dead. There was going to be a big shift in power. Would the Widow Manning stay around here and run things or would she sell out and bring some new people in? McGinley calculated this completely in his own terms. The widow didn't like him so when and if she took the reins, she'd undermine him for sure, eager to bring in her own lawman. But maybe she'd sell out and there wouldn't be anything to worry about. New folks presented an even murkier problem. They almost always brought in their own people. The sheriff over to Newton got his job because his uncle bought the bank and the bank was so important to Newton that the uncle was able to dictate damned near any changes he wanted. You wouldn't want to piss off the town's one and only banker, that was for sure.

McGinley was pondering all these imponderables when one of the morning deputies, still yawning, knuckle-knocked on McGinley's half-opened door and said, "She makes me want to scratch myself all over."

"Who does?"

"That Wilson woman."

"The one with the skin disease?"

"Yeah."

"What the hell's she want?"

"She says she's got information about Fargo."

"Well, I sure don't want her in my office."

"Then go out front and meet her."

"Yeah, that sounds about right." McGinley stood up, shook his head, and went up front.

Even from ten feet away, due to the morning light, he could see her disease. He swallowed and said, "Morning, Miz Wilson."

"You sure kept me waitin' long enough."

He wanted Fargo. The only way he was going to get him was to put up with Mrs. Wilson and her temper. And her smell. "We've been swamped here at the office, haven't we, deputy?"

"Swamped," said the deputy, "swamped."

"Too swamped to find the man that killed Del Manning?" Mrs. Wilson asked.

"Now, you know better than that, Miz Wilson. He's our first priority."

She put out a hand. He had never seen a palm so filthy. "I be wantin' half down first then."

"Half down?"

"The re-ward, Sheriff. Half down."

"You get the reward after we catch him."

"No, sir." She shook her witchy head. "No sir, not at all. I want half down and then I'll tell you where he is."

McGinley sighed. First he'd had to plead and

threaten to get his discount from the merchants. And now he had to stay on the good side of some batty, odoriferous female coot who wanted half of a reward without offering any evidence that she really and truly knew where Fargo was.

12

"Miz Wilson, I just can't do it. I'd have to get the money from the mayor and he won't give it to me till after we get Fargo." McGinley sweated out the frustrating conversation he was having with her. Capturing—or even better, killing Fargo—would solidify McGinley's new job as high sheriff. Who could doubt his cunning, his acumen, his skill if he brought Fargo back to town slung dead across a horse? Why, the mayor might give him one of those dinners that important people got—great hearty meals with great hearty and grateful people sitting around the long banquet table. (As long as they didn't serve Mrs. Mayor's apple strudel. Lordy Lordy that was awful.)

"Well, then I guess you don't get Fargo." She sat with her arms folded over her chest. Behind her in the doorway, ever the sly one, the day deputy was holding his nose and grinning. He was a regular clown, that one was. Of course, Mrs. Wilson *did* smell pretty bad.

"Then you give me half of it now."

"Miz Wilson, are you crazy? Where would I get money like that? I'm just a lawman."

"Ain't my problem, Sheriff. You either come up with the money or you don't get Fargo."

McGinley thought a moment. "Is there anything else you want, Miz Wilson?"

"Huh?"

"You know, something you really want that would

show my good faith—and that I could afford to buy you?"

"Nope. I want half that re-ward money right now or my lips is sealed."

"He's dangerous, Miz Wilson."

She giggled. "He ain't dangerous no more. Not where I got him."

"Everybody in town would be grateful to you."

"I hate everybody in this town. And they hate me. And no amount of re-ward money's gonna change that."

"Mike Donlon would probably write you up in the newspaper. Fact, I know he would."

"Wouldn't do me no good. I don't know how to read."

"There might even be a parade."

She sighed and when she sighed her breath was such that air seemed to catch fire for just a moment. Her breath nearly knocked McGinley down. It would be so damned easy—and pleasurable—to just pistol-whip her for a little while. But given her personality, he'd probably have to half-kill her to learn anything.

Then she said, "I guess there's one thing. Well, maybe a couple things."

McGinley leaned forward, excited. "There is?"

"I want me a hat."

"A hat?"

"A purty hat."

"A purty hat? Miz Wilson, right now we could go down the street and I'd buy you *three* purty hats."

"And then I want a dress."

"A dress, too, sure."

"And a garter."

"Fine."

"And then I want a fancy carriage."

"Well, now, a fancy carriage, we're talkin' about a lot of money here and—"

"A fancy carriage and I wanna ride up and down Main Street in it and wave to ever'body t'show 'em I'm just as good as they are."

"By the time we got all that done, Fargo could be halfway to San Francisco."

"Then we better not dawdle no more, should we? We should go get me a purty hat and a dress—a purty one—and a garter—a purty one of them, too—and then a fancy carriage and then we should ride up and down the street—I want you sittin' right up there with me and then we'll go get Fargo."

"But Miz Wilson—"

She stood up. She looked so eager now she almost seemed human to him. He even felt a little sorry for her. Riding up and down the main street in a fancy new dress waving to people. Like royalty. Everybody had daydreams like that—wanting not only to feel important but to feel that people saw you finally for what you really were inside, a worthy and decent human being they should like and respect. Everybody needed to feel important at least a couple of times in their lives. Even if the feeling didn't last long. Even if they went right back to being unimportant again. Even if you were Miz Wilson and a crazy woman and a walking cesspool of disease, disuse, and debilitation.

He stood up now, too. "All right. But I can't afford to buy the fancy carriage. I'll have to rent it from the livery."

"But I don't have to give the dress back, do I?"

God, he thought, who'd want to wear a dress that had been next to her flesh. Then he felt sort of ashamed of himself for having such an uncharitable thought.

Fargo had scanned the loft, the doors, and the stalls, searching for the best way to make an escape. What it came down to was that no matter which route he planned to take, he'd still have to get by Lester here. Dumb as he looked in that pitiful dress, Fargo had no doubt that he would be happy to kill him on the spot. Just as Fargo would kill Lester if he had to.

Fargo figured he could try and rush the guy but the

chances of actually grabbing the rifle before getting his head blown off were fifty-fifty at best.

By this time, the whole barnyard was alive. Cows, chickens, pigs wandering around in the midmorning sun while Fargo and Sandra were held down inside the barn by Lester.

A horse started neighing in pain. Keeping his rifle pointed straight at Fargo, Lester gave the horse some kind of medicine that seemed to calm the animal down right away.

Then Lester remembered that he had to give two other horses oats in their stalls. So he took care of that.

And then the neighbor came by.

Lester stood just inside the barn door warning the visitor not to come in because he himself had something " 'tagious." Fargo guessed he meant *con*tagious. The visitor, who didn't sound much smarter than Lester, apparently knew the family well enough to stay away from inside the barn and the 'tagious.

Not that this stopped the visitor from talking. The sonofabitch must've talked half an hour and Lester talked right back. Subjects included politics, the best way to plow, corn liquor, good Indians and bad Indians, gout, shingles, horses, the local newspaper, the new parson, and the rowboat the visitor had bought.

Just when Fargo figured it was time to make his move, Lester would glance away from the unseen visitor and redouble his aim with the rifle. Fargo would be forced to shrink back.

The visitor finally left. Fargo knew that, by this time, Ma would have reached town, told McGinley where he could find the wanted man, and was now heading up a thunderous posse going straight for her ranch.

The sick horse began wailin' again so Lester went back into the stall to see what was wrong.

Fargo and Sandra just frowned at each other. Lester was a dope but he was a fast dope. They tried anything, anything at all, he'd cut them down on the spot.

And that was when he heard the horses, Fargo did. Hard to tell how many of them there were. A good number to be sure.

And all of a sudden, they stopped.

Not too difficult to know *why* they stopped. Because McGinley would have told them to. He would also have told them to dismount and fan out around the front and the back of the farm. And then he would have said not to fire until you got a good clean shot at Fargo. *You only wound the sumbitch, he's liable to get away. You heard them stories about him and all, fightin' all five of them grizzlies at the same time. So you got to be careful. Real careful.*

Of course, McGinley would want the kill for himself if he could finagle it that way. As the new sheriff with lots of doubts about him in the town, killing the man who killed Del Manning would make for one hell of a lasting first impression. How about them apples? Anybody who thought that McGinley wasn't as good as the last sheriff—well, they were just obviously mistaken, right?

Lester stepped back into the barn, walked over to a stall, and looked down at the sick horse. "Poor boy. I shouldn't 've give him that corn liquor."

"Corn liquor? You gave a horse corn liquor?" Sandra said.

"Well, he was ailin' or somethin'—he sure *sounded* like he was ailin' anyway—so I figured that the corn liquor would kinda relax him and maybe put him to sleep."

"It'd put him to sleep, all right," Sandra said. "You could've killed him."

"Could've killed who?" Ma said, tottering through the open barn door. "Nobody's gonna kill nobody around here." She addressed Fargo. "I decided not to tell the sheriff about you."

"That's sure a purty new dress, Ma," Lester said, a certain air of possessiveness in his voice. "Where'd you git it?"

"You never mind where I got it," she snapped. Then to Fargo: "Why don't you walk outside with me a minute, Fargo. I want t'talk to ya."

So that was the setup. She would woo him outside and a couple of sharpshooters among the posse would cut him down.

"Fine, Ma. You want to go out the front door or the back?" Fargo said.

Ma couldn't help but smirk a little. Damned dummy, he could hear her thinking. All them stories about him bein' so smart and so tough. And hell he's walkin' right into the trap I set for him.

If there had been any pity in Ma except for herself, she would have felt sorry for him being so dumb and all.

But there was no pity in Ma in general and no pity in Fargo right now, either. He had to take the first chance offered him and it came when Ma held her hand out and said, "You gimme that gun now, Lester."

The first and likely the only chance Fargo would have.

Had to be exactly the right moment. When Ma had one hand on the rifle and Lester had one, too. In that second, neither would have the chance to fire.

Fargo leapt at them. Grabbed the center of the rifle in both hands and ripped the weapon free.

Sandra was at his side instantly. "Thank God."

"Don't get too happy yet," Fargo said. "I wasn't kidding about that posse."

"He sure as hell wasn't," Ma said. "Them boys is ringed all around here, just waitin' for you to come out."

"What'll we do now, Fargo?" Sandra said. She had slipped back into her princess mode. She sounded as if the entire universe—which, of course, worshiped at her feet—had utterly let her down.

Fargo had gotten used to her slightly superior ways but the way she'd whined reminded him all over again why he hadn't liked her in the first place. "You just stick by me," he said.

"Are we going somewhere?"

"Yeah. All four us."

"What the hell you talkin' about?" Ma snapped.

"I'm gonna do just what you were gonna do, Ma. I'm gonna march myself right out there. Except instead of me going first, you and Lester here are gonna go first."

"They'll just start shootin'," Ma said.

"You mean they'll kill us, Ma?"

"What the hell you think I mean, you stupid boy? 'Course they'll kill us. And if they don't, Fargo will. He's gonna use us as hostages."

"As what?" Lester said.

Fargo could see why Ma got pretty frustrated with Lester here.

"Hostages, you simp. That means he's gonna tell the posse that he'll kill us if'n they don't give Fargo and this woman here free passage."

"Oh," Lester said. He didn't sound as if he understood, but it was clear that Ma wasn't going to explain it to him again.

"How many men we talking about, Ma?" Fargo asked.

"Ten."

"Rifles?"

"Rifles and shotguns."

"How close are they?"

"They're all over the back yard. Maybe fifteen yards away behind the hay wagon."

"That'd be five. Where're the other five?"

"Behind the trees in the front of the place. Them pines."

"How'd you leave it with them?"

She shrugged. "Told them Lester had the drop on you. Told them we'd bring you out at gunpoint. I was s'posed to yell out which door we was comin' out so McGinley can get in place. He wants to show off for the townfolks."

"You go show Sandra where our guns are, Lester," Fargo said.

"I don't do nothin' lest Ma tells me to."

She sighed. "Do it, Lester."

The next few minutes were spent with Fargo walking back and forth between the barn doors to see which exit offered the best opportunity for escape. Probably the rear door. There was timber very near the wagon the five men were hiding behind, meaning they could disappear faster. The posse would have to work its way through the closely gathered jack pines to find them. The front exit was just too open. And then they'd have to swing back to get their horses anyway, traveling along the side of the barn for at least three or four minutes, making themselves extremely vulnerable.

He went to the front door a last time. "McGinley, listen to me. I'm only saying this once. We're going out the back door here. We'll have guns on Ma and Lester. Any of your men fire even one shot, we kill these two on the spot. They may not be important to you but likely some of the people in town won't be happy that you were so fired up to get me that you killed two innocent people to do it. I'm givin' you a couple minutes to think it over and to warn off your men. And then we're comin' out. From now on, the way things go is entirely up to you. You understand me?"

"You sonofabitch!" McGinley shouted.

"I'll take that as a yes."

He walked back into the shadows of the barn.

"He gonna get us killed, ain't he, Ma?"

She just scowled.

"You ready?" Fargo asked Sandra.

"You sure this is the only way we can get free?"

"If you've got a better idea, now's the time to say it."

"I just—what if they start shooting?"

"Then they start shooting."

"They wouldn't strike a deal or anything?"

He almost felt sorry for her. She obviously knew what they were up against. There was a very good chance that all four of them would be gunned down the moment they walked out the door.

Just then one of the horses in the stalls whinnied. The morning had been so tense that the horses hadn't been let out.

The moment the horse made the noise, an image came to Fargo . . . Ma and Lester walking out of the barn with their hands held high in the air, pleading for the posse members not to shoot at them and then right behind them—

Being part of a posse was fun until it came to waiting. There was nothing like the bonding of men who longed to kill somebody and be legal while they were doing it. There was also nothing like the bonding of men who liked to sit around saloons and tell each new generation how it was to track down and kill one of the most dangerous men who'd ever lived . . . *the very same fella who had killed six grizzlies that had attacked him. Or was it nine grizzlies? Whatever, this here fella was the baddest of the bad, and it was my bullets that brought him down. Yep, I drew bead on that sumbitch and just keep shootin' till he dropped.*

A lot of fun . . . except for the waiting.

Waiting in the scorching sun behind some wagon.

Waiting while about all you could do was scratch your crotch and pick your nose and wipe the sweat off your face. And watch that damned barn door.

'Course it would all be worth it if you actually got to kill the bastard. None of the posse men watching the rear door of the barn had ever known that particular pleasure, the taking of another human life, but from everything they'd heard in the saloons, you weren't quite a man until you'd put somebody six feet under. Of course, every once in a while you wondered if the saloon talker was telling the truth—there was never any way of checking up on what a man said while he was drinking away the night in a saloon—but it was more fun to assume he *was* being truthful because that made his tales so much the better.

A lot of fun . . . except for the waiting.

"Ya think Lester'll be wearin' a dress?" one of the men whispered to another.

"Prob'ly."

Another one laughed quietly. "He looks better in a dress than his ma does."

"You see that fancy one McGinley got her?"

"Yeah. But there ain't nothin' she can do for that diz-ease she got all over her face."

"I still say he's funnin' us. I bet he don't put on them dresses 'less he knows somebody's a-comin' to visit them."

"Nope. Vince Daly hunts out here and he says he sees Lester in a dress all the time. And it's when Lester don't know nobody's around."

And so it went.

One hour of talk like this. And the picking of the noses and scratching of the crotches. And the keeping of a dull, bored eye on the rear door of the barn.

And then it happened.

Here came Ma and Lester—Lester in this sad old patched-up dress and Ma in all her fancy new finery—right out into the open, they did, with their hands up shouting, "Don't shoot! Don't shoot!"

And then Fargo and the lady came out, too.

Oh, did they come out.

On a pair of bareback black horses that looked every bit as mean as Fargo did.

Firing round after round at the wagon the men were hiding behind. So that not a single one of the men had the nerve to stand up and fire back. Not with all those bullets flying around, they didn't. You wanted to live long enough to stand around a saloon and tell your story about the day you laid the Trailsman low, didn't you?

Smell of gunsmoke, roar of bullets being propelled. Shouts of posse, neigh of horses. Pounding of hooves, cry of a posseman wounded in the shoulder.

The air itself was blue with gunsmoke, the ground

itself was trembling with the thunder of the two horses going at breakneck speed.

And Fargo and the lady seeming to come straight at them. Blasting away nonstop. But just before they reached the wagon, they suddenly veered right, heading for the heavy forest in which they'd tied their own horses. Right into the woods where it would be a bitch to find them, that was for sure.

And then, to add to all the noise and confusion, the men who'd been out front were now running into sight, their own guns spewing bullets everywhere and anywhere. The possemen didn't have any idea who they were shooting at or why but they had to fire at something, didn't they, if they wanted to be true possemen? And so, guns a-blazing as they liked to say in the dime novels, they came barreling ass-over-appetite up to the wagon where the back door posse was trying to make sense of it all.

And McGinley shouting over and over again, "Where the hell's Fargo? Where the hell's Fargo?"

A man used to living by his wits, his fists, and his guns can get downright ornery when he has to put up with all the nonsense Fargo had in the past forty-eight hours, the sombrero in particular. He was a big admirer of Mexicans and Mexican culture—some of his best times had been spent in that vast and varied land—but he did not like skulking about in disguises. There was something silly and unmanly about it. He wouldn't do it again. He was going to find the person who'd killed Manning and he was going to find the gold and he was going to do both on his own terms.

All this was tucked somewhere in his mind as he came charging out of the barn on the bare back of the black horse. He was surprised to see that Sandra Evans seemed to be just as pissed off and pent up as he was. She rode easy and confident and she fired her pistol the same way.

On the muggy air, the smell of all the drifting blue

gun smoke invigorated Fargo. He'd forgotten how intoxicating it could be.

Then Fargo and Sandra were cutting wide of the wagon and heading for the trees that lay a good quarter mile past the wagon. Even though the possemen at the wagon turned now to fire at the backs of Fargo and Sandra, their intended victims were already out of range of the pistols and were only a few yards away from being out of range of the rifles.

Fargo could hear the front yard posse joining the fray. The gunshots doubled in number and volume. But they were symbolic at best. No way could they hit Fargo and Sandra now.

The sweet scent of pine and the sudden shadows of the forest introduced them abruptly to a different world. Even the sounds of the posse were muffled as they tried to penetrate the woods.

They dropped from their horses when they reached the fork in the trail where their own horses waited.

Now, the sounds of the posse were louder. The men had apparently reached the edge of the woods.

Fargo and Sandra jumped on their own horses. Fargo was in the lead. He led them quickly down the trail which was becoming a maze of shadow and sunbeams broken on the treetops. It was good to be on his Ovaro stallion again. The animal obviously sensed the danger its master was in and responded accordingly by obeying quickly every signal Fargo gave it. Low-hanging pine branches slapped the faces of horse and horseman alike but they didn't persuade either to slow down. The stallion was operating at top speed given the confines of the trail and the roughness of the terrain.

Sandra obviously knew better than to say anything. Why alert the posse to their location? The horses probably made noise enough. Fargo checked on her sometimes, making sure that she was all right. He had started liking her again. She hadn't played the princess once since they'd come racing out of the barn.

The clearing they came to was a surprise. Even

more surprising was the river that lay close by. Fargo's stallion began moving even faster toward the water. At the edge of the river, Fargo dropped from his animal and ran for a look at the river. The water was so pure he could see the bottom. They wouldn't have any trouble crossing it.

On the other side, they headed straight for a ring of foothills to the west. Scrub pine covered the hills. There would be even more and better hiding places there. And then, come night, Fargo was going to double back and pay certain people in town some surprise visits. He was hungry for a conclusion now. And eager to settle up with whomever had forced him to become a fugitive.

Side by side they rode toward the foothills. Fargo was hoping that they'd have a little private time to themselves. He hadn't gotten enough of her that first and only time. Even a fugitive was entitled to a little fun once in a while.

13

Fargo waited for the moon.

It came early this time of year, even before full dark.

He sat on an outcropping that allowed him to see the valley floor below. The posse had come this way several hours ago but had turned in the wrong direction. He wanted to talk to Lala Huang and Faye Manning. They were both suspects to him now that he'd learned about the gold. He wanted to confront Lala to see exactly what she knew. Faye might know where the gold was, too.

The problem with Faye Manning was getting into the mansion. He imagined that they'd been able to limit the fire to the den, keeping the rest of the place inhabitable. She would likely have loaded up on gunnies to keep safe. Or, knowing Faye, to take a couple upstairs to use for her own amusement as well.

A quarter moon imposed itself through the clouds and sky and as if honoring its sudden presence, a wolf silhouetted against the dying day began to cry in a lonely but elegant way.

"You're really going to leave me behind?"

"Yep."

"That's not fair, Fargo."

She sat down next to him on the outcropping. "I'm to just sit here and wait till you get back?"

"If I get back. They'll shoot me on sight now. And they'll kill you right along with me."

"I can take care of myself."

"Yeah, but I'd worry about you. And that'd distract me."

"You're a pretty selfish man. You wouldn't worry about me at all. You'd worry about *you* worrying about me."

He laughed. "I guess I never thought of it that way before."

"That comes from living alone too long. You become your only concern."

"You'll just get in the way, I'm sorry."

They were silent for a time.

The wolf cried again.

"I feel like he does," she said quietly.

"Yeah, I get that way myself sometimes."

"That's hard to believe. Given your reputation and all."

"You mean all those grizzlies I killed barehanded?"

"And saving that steamboat from going over the falls that time."

"Now that one I hadn't heard."

"You mean you didn't do it?"

"*Some*body might have done it. But it wasn't me."

"You mean people make *up* stories about you?"

"Sure. And not just me. They make 'em up about a lot of people."

"But why?"

He shrugged. "I guess they like to think that somewhere out there there're people who aren't like average folks. They're smarter and deadlier and better looking and never get scared or sick or lonely. I s'pose it gives 'em hope."

"Hope for what?"

"Oh, you know, that someday this hero'll come into their lives and straighten it up for them. Show them how to never get scared or sick or lonely. Show them how to be a hero. And besides, it's fun to sit around and talk about them. All the derring-do stuff."

She laughed. "Like holding off ten grizzlies."

"Now I thought it was twenty."

"And I'll bet you did it right on the deck of that steamboat you were saving from going over the falls."

"I sure did. And damned if those Injuns didn't attack at just about the same time."

They both had the same idea, the Lord be praised.

He took her gentle this time. It was probably that stupid quarter moon and that silly damned musical wolf and all that talk about how real ordinary everyday people—just like them—really do get scared and lonely a lot, even if they won't admit it to anybody but themselves.

They didn't talk as they rode toward town. They let the night take them, a suddenly chill night for this time of year, a comfortable and welcome chill after the heat. They stopped at the junction of two stage roads and spent a few minutes talking in the shadowed beauty of the starlight.

"What if they kill you, Fargo?"

"Then they kill me. I don't plan to go through life with a murder charge on my head."

"I'll keep trying to find out what happened even if—even if you're not around to help me."

"I appreciate that."

"I wish I was as fearless as you."

"Nobody's fearless. Hell, I don't want to die. I'm just damned mad is all. And there's so much mad in my brain there isn't any room for fear right now. But about the time I hit the town limits, I'll start gettin' a little bit nervous."

"You will?"

"Hell, yes, I will. But then I'll start thinkin' about that murder charge again and my nerves'll go away."

"Good luck."

"Just don't do anything stupid. You gave me your word you wouldn't sneak into town after me."

"I won't. I promise."

Fargo nodded, reined his stallion in the direction of the stage road, and headed off into the early night.

* * *

When she opened the door, Lala Huang jerked back in surprise if not outright shock. "They're looking for you."

"I know," Fargo said and slipped inside her tiny rented rooms. The air smelled of fresh tea. A lantern pulsed light into the small living quarters. Lala Huang wore a silk robe that did things most pleasing to her diminutive but perfect body.

"You should not be here, Skye. Everybody in town is looking for you. There is a very large reward."

"In case you're wondering, Lala, I didn't kill Del Manning."

"No, then who did?" She went over to the stove where the teakettle had begun to whistle. "You would like some tea?"

"No, thanks."

She poured tea into a dainty, flower-painted cup and then sat on the small couch with Fargo. "You took a big chance coming here."

He said, "Why didn't you tell me about the gold?"

For a second, guilt or shock stunned her dark, lovely gaze. That second was all it took for Fargo to see that she did indeed know about the gold. Or was he imagining it? You had to be careful. Sometimes your mind tricked you, told you what you wanted to see even if it wasn't there. His presence had surprised her. She was no doubt still confused and anxious over the death of her brother. She probably wasn't in control of her reactions.

On the other hand, she could damned well be lying.

At times like these, Fargo realized how much faces were like masks. You had to be careful what you chose to see in them. They could mislead the hell out of you.

"I do not understand what you say, Skye." She put the lie forth in a suddenly heavy accent. The poor, sweet-faced Chinese waif. The perfect victim pose to tame the brash American brawler who had suspicions about her. Or was she being perfectly honest? If anybody had the right to strike a victim pose, it was certainly Lala Huang. She'd been through hell these past few days.

"You said Huang Chow told you he was coming into money."

"Yes, he did say that."

"Did he say anything more?"

She thought a moment. "Not really."

"Anything about Li Ping?"

"No."

"Or Manning?"

"Del Manning? Why would he say anything about Del Manning? You mean he stole from Mr. Manning?"

"He stole, all right. But not *from* Mr. Manning. *For* Mr. Manning. And Li Ping helped him."

He told her everything he'd learned, watching her closely as he spoke. She was strangely silent. She sat primly, the tea cup in the palm of one slight, upturned hand. And then with no warning, tears began tracing the angles of her cheek bones, glimmering in the lantern light.

When she finally spoke, he could barely hear her. She said, "Huang Chow was not a good son. He disgraced my father's house."

"Yeah, I guess he did."

"In the old country, he would be driven from our family home."

"How bad did he beat you?"

She hesitated. Glanced down at her tea cup. "That does not matter now."

"I'd like to know."

She raised her eyes to his. "He is dead. Let him rest."

He shrugged. "All right."

She stood up abruptly, went to the window. "I'm glad it's night, Skye. He comes to me at night. Or do you not believe in ghosts?"

"Sometimes I do, I guess."

"He has asked for forgiveness. And I have already

forgiven him. That is why I don't wish to defame him anymore."

Fargo got up and walked over to her. The stars were out full and bright now. He had the sense that she was like him, that she could study the stars and moon as long as he did. There was peace in such stargazing.

"Did he have any favorite hiding places? Ever mention anything like that?"

"Hiding places." She paused. "No, I don't think so."

"The gold. That's what whoever killed Manning is looking for. I thought that maybe your brother might have hidden it somewhere for Manning."

"I don't know of any such hiding places, Skye. I'm sorry."

"Did he leave anything stored here?"

"No. It was all out at Manning's, where he stayed. In the servants' quarters there."

A second reason to visit the mansion tonight. He'd turned back to the couch when he realized that the small black statue of an Asian deity was missing from its table. "Say, where's my statue?"

She didn't understand his reference. "Statue?"

"The little black one."

"Oh." She forced a smile. "I wasn't sure what you meant. I probably shouldn't flaunt being Asian."

He felt sorry for her as he did most Chinese immigrants. The West hadn't been kind to them. Being kind seemed a long ways off, in fact.

"I was dusting and knocked it over and it broke. I had to throw her out."

"Goddesses don't take kindly to treatment like that."

"The next time I am in San Francisco, I will buy you one, Skye. You can keep her with you for luck."

They both knew that her offer was formal and empty. Fargo would be long gone—either by hangman's rope or horse—by the time she went to San Francisco and back.

"Why don't you get me two of them?" he joked. "That'll be for even better luck."

He picked up his hat.

"I'm afraid for you, Skye. You should leave this town. Go somewhere else fast before McGinley catches you."

"Not with a murder charge hanging over my head. I don't want to leave with a bounty on me. I like to enjoy myself. I'd hate having to look over my shoulder all the time."

"But McGinley—well, I don't have to tell you what kind of man McGinley is."

"No, you don't. But I can't back off now. I think I'm getting close. I'm getting the sense that Faye Manning never told me the truth about anything. I'm going out there as soon as I finish up at the livery stable."

"Is something wrong with that beautiful horse of yours?"

"A bad shoe. I'm not going to make him work on it anymore."

"But the liveryman, won't he—"

"He won't go for McGinley as long as I'm holding a gun on him. Probably won't take long and then I can get away. Then it doesn't matter what he tells McGinley."

She came into his arms, hugged him tight. "You've helped me so much, Skye. I wish there was some way I could help you."

He held her away from him, grinned. "Just get me that statue of that naked lady."

She grinned back. "Two statues, remember? *Two* naked ladies."

14

Fargo had always liked liveries. They were a man's province. He enjoyed the jokes, the gossip, the tobacco smoke, the skill and craft of the blacksmith.

This particular livery wasn't in danger of becoming one of his favorite places. The small man who appeared in a nightshirt carrying a lantern had one of the owliest faces Fargo had ever seen. Not even the man's dopey night cap added a friendly touch.

"I got a cold."

"Good for you," Fargo said. "I got a horse needs some help."

"Come back in the morning. You got any idea what time it is?"

"Yeah. About nine o'clock."

"Middle of the night."

"Not where I come from."

It was then the small man recognized him. "You're Fargo."

Fargo let him see his Colt. "And you're in a lot of trouble unless you take care of my horse."

The livery was a barn and a shack, the latter being the place where the blacksmith lived.

Fargo led the stallion over to the work area inside the barn. Then he rolled himself a cigarette and watched as the small man went to work on the shoe. The whole time he worked, the man muttered to himself.

"Share some of those words with me."

"Why the hell should I?"

"I want to see if you're plottin' anything against me."

"Won't have to. McGinley's got such a hate for you, he'll shoot you on sight."

"For what it's worth, I didn't kill Manning."

"I don't expect you to admit it."

"How we coming?"

"We're coming just fine. I've shoed a few horses in my time, mister. This ain't exactly difficult work."

"You always this cranky?"

The man paused with his hammer in midair. "I'm half this cranky when my gout's actin' up."

"Oh, yeah?"

"I'm only this cranky when the gout *and* the hemorrhoids is actin' up together. And sometimes when the gout and the hemorrhoids and the shingles all get goin' together—well, you don't want to be nowhere around me. Not even if you do have your gun. That only happened once and I took it out on Mrs. Manning."

"How'd she handle it?"

"That was the funny thing. She had that Chinee with her and they both looked sorta scared or somethin'. Didn't pay no attention to how cranky I got. I was a swearin' and a wailin' and they kind of whispered back and forth between themselves. He paced while the Manning woman sat fidgetin' with her hands."

Fargo didn't get the last part clearly because just then his stallion protested getting shoed, the way horses sometimes did for seemingly no reason at all.

"You hold still, boy," Fargo said, going over to his old friend. "We'll be out of here right soon."

And then he was done. "There you go, mister."

"How much?"

"You gonna pay me?"

"You did the job, didn't you?"

"Yeah, but I figured you bein' a killer and all—"

"I told you I didn't kill him."

"Yeah, but killers always say they didn't kill so-and-so. And nobody believes 'em. Not even when they say it right before they hang."

"Well, for what it's worth, Manning got himself killed by somebody else."

The little man actually seemed curious. "Who you think killed him—I mean, sayin' I go along with your story that you didn't?"

"That's what I'm gonna find out tonight."

"And jes' how'll you do that?"

Fargo laughed. "That's the part I haven't come up with yet."

Fargo took the long way around to the Manning place. All the usual guards would be posted at their various sentry posts. Just because Del Manning was dead didn't mean that his gunnies wouldn't be protecting the place. From what he'd seen of Faye Manning, she could run the place as ruthlessly as her husband had.

He came in from the east side of the sprawling grounds, tying his stallion to a birch tree that glowed in the moonlight, and crouching down for his long run to the sentry post on this side of the estate.

The first man he'd have to get past was a tall, slim man in work clothes and chaps. He toted a Henry much like Fargo's own. Fargo watched him for ten minutes from the edge of a small trench that had been dug for ranch work. The man walked his beat without much interest. His posture was bad and a couple of times he paused to yawn. Fargo didn't blame the man. This had to be one of the dullest jobs around.

Fargo was about to make his run when another sentry came around the far side of the house. This man was short, wide, and bald. The two men laughed about something and then talked for a few minutes. Then the short one went back to his post on the other side of the mansion. The men had a dull job walking post. Fargo had a dull job *watching* them walk post.

Then it was time for him to do what he needed to do. Any other time, he might have been a mite nervous. But not now. He was thankful the waiting and the boredom were over.

Faye Manning had spent the day in town preparing her husband's funeral. Much as she'd despised him, she needed to play the dutiful wife of the most powerful man in the area. He would be buried with the courtly rights of an emperor. The funeral home people would have a fancy carriage shipped in from San Francisco. An orator who pretended to be a minister would also be brought in. And a chorus comprised of young girls in black dresses and garlanded hair would also come. This would delay the funeral by several days. As a result, they'd put the corpse in an ice house so that it wouldn't smell unduly when they coffined it into the church. A foul odor could, after all, overpower even the most imposing of funeral ceremonies.

The rest of the day she'd made sure that her sentries were rested, sober, and eager to win the promised thousand dollar reward for shooting and killing Skye Fargo on sight. There was good reason for this. She had no doubt he was in the area. He wasn't the type of man who'd run out on a murder charge. He'd want to clear his name. And in doing so, his path would eventually bring him here, to the mansion and to Faye. As the beneficiary of Del's will, she'd certainly inherited a pleasing sum of money and property. But the money wasn't anywhere near sufficient to the need she had—she needed to live in luxury for the rest of her life. And the property; that could take forever to dispose of. The national economy was about to enter another recession. Land values would diminish and so would the number of available buyers. While many investors bought property during bad times, Del's spread wasn't going to get them the kind of quick payback they'd want.

And that's what she wanted, too. The quick payback. So her plan was simple. She would convert everything she could into cash and then in a month or two she would tell the townsfolk, who might have the temerity to ask her, that she was going to visit a sick relative. After that she'd never see them or the town again. She couldn't live among rubes much longer.

And just before she left, she would arrange to have the gold shipped to the house she'd buy in San Francisco. Of course, the gold would have to be concealed inside of something to avoid suspicion. But that could be worked out.

Leaving only Fargo to worry about.

She knew he'd be here and she knew it would probably be tonight. Hiram had told her of Fargo's visit and how determined he was to clear his name.

The mansion still smelled of smoke from the den fire the other night. She thus spent most of her time on the second floor, in her rooms. She'd even started taking her meals here. She had packed one derringer up the sleeve of her summer-weight organdy dress and another down the side of her shoe. For all her anxiety, though, there was still some playfulness in her. She imagined what it would be like to seduce Fargo before she killed him. Work him like a sex slave, leave him so exhausted that he couldn't possibly put up a fight when she took out her derringer and shot him in the heart.

The image amused her as she stood at the window looking out on the night. From here she could see the sentries on the west side of the house. Seeing their silhouettes—and their gleaming rifles—in the moonlight reassured her that everything would work out fine. Skye Fargo would be dead by morning. She felt certain of it.

She poured herself some brandy. Her bedroom was done in white. Del had always laughed about the "virginal" aspects of the room, especially the canopied bed. Del had snored so loudly that she'd often been "forced" to retreat to her own bed. That's the way she'd put it to him, anyway, that she only slept alone when his snoring demanded it. She preferred sleeping alone to sleeping with Del. He'd been a scratcher, a moaner, a belcher, a farter, a groaner, a leg-twitcher, and a mutterer. Every once in a while he'd even been a screamer, rising from the bed, still completely asleep, and shrieking out like a little girl at some nightmare image that was chasing him down the dark alleys of his mind.

She went back to the window.

Skye Fargo was out there somewhere in the night. He might be waiting in the woods by now, waiting for his chance to slip past the sentries and get into the mansion. She had no doubt that he would be violent this time. She'd set him up perfectly. Dumb old Sheriff McGinley hadn't questioned anything about Del's murder. Open and shut case to somebody as unimaginative as McGinley.

Good old McGinley.

She wouldn't have any trouble convincing him that she'd shot Fargo in self-defense—even if she shot him in the back.

15

Fargo was halfway to the Manning estate when he heard, somewhere in the distance behind him, the clatter of a buckboard. Since the road to the Manning place was, from this point on, seldom used by anybody except people headed to the mansion or the ranch, Fargo decided to pull off the road and hide behind a tree. He didn't doubt that he could sneak into the mansion grounds again but why bother when there was an easier way.

Moonlight. Road dust. Barn owl. Wolf cry. Heat. These were Fargo's company as he waited for the buckboard to come into sight.

It was a much larger wagon than he'd thought. No wonder it had made so much noise from such a distance.

What he was interested in now was the wagon bed. After knocking out the driver with a rock, he could always lie down in the bed and hold a gun to the man's back when he woke up. That was one way to get on to the grounds.

A better way was to knock the man out and then hide beneath a canvas-covered bed. That way the man might not even see Fargo at all. And he couldn't warn anybody once Fargo crept out of the wagon and raced to the mansion.

Fargo started his search for a good-sized rock. It took him longer than he'd thought. He was either getting slower or the wagon was getting faster. Whichever, he'd barely had time to assume his position behind the tree when the wagon pulled abreast of him.

There was only one man, which was good. And from the stupid song he was singing off-key—something about a heavyset one-eyed whore, the kind of song sailors sang—he sounded pretty drunk, which was even better.

Fargo hurled the rock with enough force to send pain shooting up his right arm. The driver wasn't wearing a hat, which was damned nice of him. The rock got him in the middle of the back of his head. About all he had time to do was send a loud curse across the tree-lined landscape and then fall over on his side.

Fargo's luck didn't hold. There was no canvas covering on the wagon bed.

He jumped on his stallion, rode fast to catch up with the wagon, leaned over and grabbed the bridle on the horse, pulling the vehicle to a stop.

He dropped down from his stallion to see how the man was doing. He was already groaning, which meant he wouldn't be out long.

Fargo climbed up onto the front of the wagon, grabbed the stout man's hair, and pulled him up into a sitting position.

"What the hell happened?" The man groaned, touching a hand to the back of his head. "Hey, you sonofabitch, I'm bleedin' and this is a brand-new shirt. How come you knocked me out, anyway?"

"Because you sing so bad."

"You bastard," the man said, not finding Fargo especially funny. Maybe if he hadn't had a pounding headache, a bloody head, and a ruined new shirt he would have seen some humor. But not right now. The man was patting around on the back of his shirt. "It's all soaked with blood."

Fargo wondered if the driver was still so drunk he didn't realize that somebody had hijacked his wagon and he was instead chiefly concerned with his new shirt.

"You're taking me into the mansion."

"Hey, I know who you are."

"I know who I am, too."

"You're the gent what killed Del Manning."

"I didn't but I don't expect you to believe me."

"Hell, man, I'd be happy to buy you a drink. I worked for him for six years and he never said a kind word to me once." He touched his head. "I don't suppose you'd let me bean *you* with a rock, would ya?"

"Not right now, I'm afraid."

"I hate holdin' grudges. All you do is sit around and stew about people you hate. But if you could settle the score, you wouldn't stew about 'em no more. You'd have time to set your mind t'other things."

Fargo smiled. "And here I thought *I* was crazy." He nodded to the horse. "I'm going to ride alongside you for another half mile or so. Then I'm going to hide my horse and lay down in the bed back there. I'll have a gun on you the whole time. You try anything, I'll shoot you."

"Shoot me dead?"

"Well, shoot you at least so you'll *wish* you were dead," Fargo said. "Now let's roll."

Faye Manning had decided to review the troops.

She swept down the front steps of the mansion and began walking around the grounds to make sure that each man was in his place, sober, and paying attention to his post.

Her fate rested in the hands of uncouth, uneducated, unfriendly men who would rob, rape, and perhaps kill her if they ever got the chance. But their proclivity toward barbarism was exactly what she wanted in guards. She just hoped they would visit it on Fargo when he showed up and leave her alone.

The night was cooling at last. The lowing of cattle and sound of horses settling into their stalls was friendly and relaxing. Animals had always pleased her far more than humans. Humans were likely to betray you—wasn't she herself a betrayer?—while animals you could cajole into doing exactly what you wanted. And if you couldn't cajole them, you could always beat the hell out of them. And then they'd be submissive.

"Evening, ma'am," the guard said.

"Evening. No sign of Fargo?"

"Nope. I reckon he's too smart to come out here. He knows what'll happen to him if he does." He pridefully patted his rifle.

"That's what you reckon, is it?"

"Yes, ma'am." But his voice was leery now. He obviously sensed that she was irritated. As she usually was. You never knew what to say to this woman without somehow pissing her off.

"Well, you reckon wrong."

"Yes, ma'am."

"Because I reckon he reckons that if he could sneak in here once—the way he did the last time—then he can do it again so maybe the next time you *reckon* something, I *reckon* you'd best keep your stupid mouth shut, because I *reckon* you're full of shit."

She wasn't much nicer to the other guards. They were all under the impression that with top guns like themselves involved, there was no way Fargo could get on to the grounds. What they lacked in modesty, they more than made up for in stupidity, just like Stan. If a fellow could sneak in once, wasn't there at least the possibility that he could sneak in again?

She went back into the house. She had been looking through a crudely printed history of this region earlier in the day and had found it relaxing. The common folks weren't named, they were just alluded to as "fine loyal Americans." All they did, of course, was clear the land, build the dams, irrigate the farmland, see that at least primitive schools were built, and keep their towns safe when marauding gangs tried to take them over.

The prominent people on the other hand—the people she identified with—were the ones who held dances, went back East whenever possible, entertained other prominent people in their mansions, hired snooty maids and servants from Chicago, put on musicals with their own dear sweet spoiled children as the stars, and gave all the commoners some small, very small, token of their esteem when Christmas rolled around. There were ten families with family histories in the book. Almost all of them had trekked from the East with money in tow, wanting to start new lives on the frontier.

So now, as she waited, a pistol on the table before her, she pored over the book and knew that, unlike most of the people mentioned here, she'd come from nothing. Her own personal history was so much more fascinating than theirs. But given that that history involved various kinds of crimes and moral failings, it was probably best not to put it into print anywhere.

Just the number of men she'd slept with while married to Del would curl the hair of every parson this side of the Mississippi.

16

"I'm still bleedin'," the wagon driver said. "And it's soakin' into my shirt."

"I'll tell you what, I'll give you a little money and you buy yourself a new one, how's that?"

"You serious?"

"Yep."

"Well, that'd be right nice of you."

"But you gotta do one thing for me."

"Yeah? And what'd that be?"

"You gotta shut up about it."

The driver laughed over his shoulder so he could be heard by Fargo, who lay in the bed of the wagon. "I drivin' you crazy, am I?"

"You sure as hell are."

They rode the rest of the way in silence.

When Fargo raised himself up to see what lay ahead, he got his first glimpse of the Manning place.

He had two things to fear now. One was that the driver would give some kind of signal to the guard at the front gate that Fargo was in the bed. The other was that the guard wouldn't need a signal, he'd just see Fargo for himself.

Fargo tensed, got himself ready for either eventuality. He gripped his Colt even harder. Ready, now; ready.

To remind the driver that he was back there, Fargo reached his gun hand up and put the tip of the barrel at the small of the man's back. Neither man said anything. Nothing needed to be said.

Fargo had to lie flat again as the wagon started to slow, now that it was coming up to the gate.

"Evenin', Henry," the driver said. "Pass me on through."

"You gonna make me get up? I been standin' for the last four hours. Just now sat down."

Fargo pictured the gate setup. The long, chest-high metal gate that swung open from the right.

"Ain't locked," the guard said from some distance. "Your horse can nuzzle it open."

Fargo listened hard for any innuendo—any hint of something wrong—in the driver's voice. Some signal to the guard. Wasn't much Fargo could do if the driver decided to signal with his eyes. Fargo figured that the guard was far enough away so he could roll over, facing upward, his gun ready, in case the guard came up to the wagon bed suddenly.

Crickets, mosquitoes, cicadas filled the night air with their natural songs as Fargo waited. The wagon horse dropped some particularly odoriferous road apples and the front seat groaned as the driver shifted position.

Fargo lay face up now. Why the hell wasn't the wagon moving?

"What's holdin' you up?" the guard asked.

Long silence. Fargo tensed. He'd thought of a third alternative. The driver could always pitch himself off the wagon and then get the guard to start pumping bullets into the wagon bed. Fargo would be trapped. You didn't find many good hiding places in an empty wagon bed.

And then the wagon moved with a slight jerk as the horse pulled ahead. Fargo could hear the gate creak open.

"See you later," the guard called in the starry gloom.

When they were past the gate, Fargo rolled over

again and said, "You almost did something stupid, didn't you?"

"Yeah, I almost did. But I figured anybody who'd pay for my shirt's probably not so bad, after all."

The shirt. My God. Half the people in this town seemed crazy to Fargo. He was eager to get back to an "uncivilized" town where everybody had the usual reasons for hating people. Cheating you at cards, sneaking off with your wife, swiping your horse, or insulting your manhood. Who the hell could get this excited, one way or the other, about a shirt?

"I want you to let me off as close to the house as you can."

"I don't usually get very close."

"You will tonight."

"If you say so, I guess."

Fargo dug some money from his buckskins. About the time he was ready to roll off the back end of the bed, he reached up and lay the money on the seat next to the driver.

"Hey, I can get me a good one with this much money."

The shirt, Fargo thought. The shirt.

He rolled off the wagon while it was still rolling. He'd timed this so he'd land just as the rear-entrance guard had started moving in the opposite direction. He paused behind the tree he'd used the other night and then made his rush for the house.

He got inside with no problem. Now was probably the riskiest time of all. Finding Faye in this maze of rooms without being spotted.

He moved, silent as he could, down the corridors of the palacelike home.

The wing of the house containing the burned-out den still smelled of smoke and water-soaked wood. The walls ranged in color from sooty gray to charred black. They'd been lucky to contain the fire as well as they had.

He went from room to room. The ground floor seemed vaster than ever. Once, he heard a servant—

or somebody—coming up from behind him. He had to take the chance and open a door and duck inside.

He heard the person going by singing. A female Spanish voice. A servant. He started his search again.

The Mexican servant came back around the corner. He ducked into another room. He feared that she'd seen him. But she seemed too interested in the laundry she was carrying to look up.

When she was gone, he opened the door and started his way to the staircase that would take him to the second floor. Another high-risk moment. Once he was on the second floor, he could easily be trapped there. Her guards, if they knew he was in here, could block him from escaping down the stairs. And they could station themselves outside in such a way to see all the windows, so there'd be no escape there, either.

He ascended the wide, sweeping staircase, angling himself so that he could easily see where he was going and where he was coming from. He didn't need anybody sneaking up behind him. Nor did he need anybody lurking in the shadows at the top of the stairs.

A few minutes later, he stood on the second floor, looking first left, then right. The hallways were as long and door-lined as the fanciest hotel he'd ever been in.

He had to find Faye Manning quickly.

She made it easy for him.

She came out of one room, grand in a dramatic organdy robe the color of the finest turquoise, and went into the next room.

He'd had time to flatten himself against the wall in a shadowy section that the flickering light from the wall sconces didn't reach.

It was time to make his move.

He listened at her door for two long minutes before even touching the doorknob. He needed to make sure that she had indeed not seen him. She was an intelligent and devious woman. She might well have set a trap for him—pretending not to have seen him, then waiting inside with a drawn pistol.

There was only one way to make sure.

He opened the door and walked in.

She sat at a beauty table, brushing her lovely blond hair. The room smelled of perfume, powder. Her image in the mirror was portraitlike, perfect. The robe had fallen to her hips, exposing her white freckled shoulders and arms and her elegantly tipped breasts. She had one of those voluptuous bodies that was as sleek and perfect as a thinner woman's. Her extra pounds did not distort her shapeliness.

She was so caught up in her own image in the mirror that she didn't notice him for a moment. And when she did notice him, she remained as calm and wry as ever. "I don't suppose you came here to make love."

"You know why I'm here, Faye."

A few more brushes of her hair. Each time she dragged the brush through her hair, her breasts rose. He couldn't help but be fascinated. He couldn't help but want to give into the heat and urgency forming in his groin.

"You snuck up behind me that night and then killed your husband."

Anybody else would have denied it. Tried to talk him out of his charge. But not Faye. She laughed. "You don't think he had it coming? All the dirty things he'd done to people over his life?"

She angled toward him, giving him a frontal view of her body. He licked his lips.

He got control of himself. "Where's the gold?"

A laugh again. "Oh, Fargo, you're so damned handsome when you're mad like this. You really are. So earnest and everything. You're like a sweet little boy—all intense about everything."

He raised his Colt.

"Oh, Lord, Fargo, don't go dramatic on me. I'm afraid you're not very good at that. You're too masculine for theatrics. You wouldn't shoot me, anyway, and we both know it."

"Put some clothes on. We're going into town."

"Oh, we are, are we?" Still sounding very amused by it all. "And how do you plan to get past my guards?"

"Tell them that if they don't let us through, I'll shoot you right on the spot."

"And you think they'll believe you?"

"I'll shoot you in the arm or the leg first. Then they'll believe me."

For just a second, he saw behind her mask. Saw the fear that his words had put in her eyes. *Shoot you in the arm or leg first.* Apparently by being so specific, she saw that he was serious.

She studied him a moment. "I guess you would, wouldn't you?"

"You don't want to take the risk and find out."

He might not have seen the dark, sculpted figure if he hadn't moved slightly to his right. But there it was on a shelf with several other similar figurines. The same small black statue that Lala Huang had in her room.

He walked over to it and picked it up. "Sometimes, I'm not as smart as I should be, but eventually I catch on. Lala Huang is in this with you?"

She stood up, gathered her robe about her. "That sweet little Chinese woman. She's awfully good at that role, don't you think?" She smiled. "We were in San Francisco together. That's where we bought the statues. Matching ones. We had the same problem, so it made sense for us to work together."

"What problem?"

"Men. Her brother was insanely jealous of her. He beat her any time he thought she was disgracing the family. Which was often. She'd tried to run away but both times he'd found her and dragged her back. The beatings just got worse. So when she found out what her brother and my husband were planning—well, we got together and planned a a little surprise for them."

She leaned over, picked up a cigarette she hadn't finished, relighted it. "I killed Li Ping that morning and made it look as if Huang Chow had done it. And then Del killed Huang Chow so he could get his share of the gold."

"Nice and tidy."

"Very."

"So who killed your husband?"

"I did," said the voice behind him.

He didn't have to turn around to know who had spoken.

"You've been nice to me, Skye. Please put your gun down so I don't have to kill you, too."

"Killing doesn't seem to be much of a problem for either of you."

"Only when it's necessary," Lala Huang said and walked over to Faye Manning. She'd crept silently in the door behind Fargo.

"Personally, I wouldn't mind killing you at all, Fargo. You're quite remarkable in the sack," Faye Manning said, "but otherwise you're something of a pest."

"Thanks for the compliment."

"Don't let it go to your head, dear."

Lala Huang walked up to Skye and took his gun from him. "You really have been very sweet."

"I'm going to start crying here in a minute," Fargo said. "First she tells me I'm good in the hay and now you're telling me I'm sweet. Hard to believe that you're both cold-blooded, ruthless killers."

"You don't understand what it's like to be a slave to somebody," Lala Huang said.

"Maybe not. But that's only part of the reason you killed them. The other part was plain, old-fashioned greed."

"If I didn't know better, Lala, I'd think he didn't like us anymore."

"I'm sorry to say this, Skye, but I'm afraid we'll have to kill you now." Lala Huang spoke so quietly and looked so shy when she said this that Fargo almost broke out laughing. Faye Manning was right. Lala Huang knew how to play the waif very, very well.

"There's a place in the basement, Lala," Faye said. "We'll take him there to shoot him. He's too heavy to lug all the way down the stairs. We can bury him there, too. There's a lime pit Del had to use a few times to take care of hired men who'd turned against him."

"I'm sorry, Skye," Lala Huang said softly.

"You're doing it again," Fargo said.

"Doing what?" Lala Huang said.

"Making me want to sit down and cry. I can tell how much you don't want to kill me."

Lala Huang smiled. "We compared notes, Faye and I. And I agree with her. You're really very good in bed."

"Well, I'm always glad to get compliments from killers."

"Too bad there isn't time to give you a proper send-off, Fargo," Faye Manning said. "You know, take us both to bed at the same time." She touched her wondrous breasts.

"Now *that* would be fun," Lala Huang said.

"Unfortunately, we have to meet the gold we sent by stage yesterday. It'll be waiting for us in San Francisco. I imagine it'll get lonely for us if we're not there to pick it up as soon as possible. I have a friend who owns a bank there, and he's agreed to help me store it, the dear. For a price, of course. But we don't mind. Everybody's selfish when you come right down to it, don't you think, Fargo?"

17

As lime pits went, it wasn't all that much. There were certainly much larger ones, there were certainly more efficient ones, there were certainly more imposing ones as to the simple *look* of the thing. For dramatic effect, this should have had some human bones, maybe even a few skulls lying about the edges of it. If you really wanted to scare the hell out of somebody, anyway.

This one covered a ten-by-ten area in the west end of the basement. A large barrel of lime with a couple of lime-tainted shovels loomed in the lantern light. The harsh odor of the stuff did quick damage to Fargo's sinuses. He teared up and started sneezing.

"I guess your body just doesn't like lime," Faye Manning said with bitchy sweetness. "You poor thing."

"I'm not sure how we do this, Faye," Lala Huang said.

Faye Manning laughed. "It's pretty simple. We push Fargo here into the lime and come back in a while to see how he's doing."

"But can't he get up from there when we're gone?"

"Not if he has a couple of bullets in his head. And I'd really like the pleasure of putting them there myself. I don't care for Mr. Fargo."

"Be my guest. I still sort of like him."

"Yeah," Fargo said, "I can see that, Lala. You letting her shoot me and all."

"My people have a saying. 'When things are out of your hands, put your hands to use on something else.' "

"Gosh, I'm getting kind of choked up. And here I thought it was the lime."

He glanced around. Being in the far corner of the massive and shadowy basement, he saw few opportunities for cover. He could race over to hide behind the stacks of boxes stored down here and then make his way to the stairs and escape. That is, if one of them didn't shoot him in the back as he was making his getaway. Faye Manning would no doubt take great pleasure in being the one who did it.

"Keep your gun on him," she said now.

Faye Manning went to the corner where she got a slender piece of wood. She came back to the lime pit and began to stir its contents. "I got this ready today. I was hoping I'd get a chance to try it out on our friend Fargo here."

When she was satisfied that the pit was ready to use, she walked back to the corner, turned around abruptly and said, "I don't want any regrets, Lala. You seem to have some unreasonable fondness for the man. I need a demonstration that you won't back out of this."

"But you said *you* wanted to shoot him."

"I do want to shoot him. The fatal shots, anyway. Bring the gun over here to me, Lala."

"But—"

Fargo could see that there was at least some doubt in Lala Huang's mind. Her dark eyes grew soft with remorse and she said, "I am sorry about this, Skye."

"Sorry enough not to shoot me?"

"I told you to bring that gun over here, Lala."

Fargo had an idea. "This is how it'll be with Faye," he said. "She'll take charge. She's probably convinced you that you'll be equal partners. But you won't be. She's already acting like your boss. And who knows, maybe she'll even try to cheat you out of the gold. Or take it all herself."

Lala glanced at Faye Manning, who said, "If you're stupid enough to fall for what he's telling you, I don't *want* you as a partner. He'll say anything, Lala. He's trying to save his life. Can't you see that?"

"Do we *have* to kill him?"

Faye Manning frowned. "This is really disgusting. We came all this way to get rich—and now you're going to let *him* stand in our way? Think it through. We'll go prison if we don't kill him. The only way he can clear his name is to turn us over. We might even hang. They do hang women, you know. So all of this will have been for nothing. We were both raised poor. We deserve our own special time. We deserve to have some fun. Your brother beat you up whenever he felt like it. And my husband tried to keep me a prisoner. Isn't it our turn to have a life, Lala?"

Fargo could see the drama playing out in Lala's mind. She didn't have any trouble condoning three other murders but for some reason she liked Fargo enough that—

She shot him in the leg. Right below the knee.

The explosive sound rumbled through the entire basement. Lala looked as surprised as Fargo and Faye Manning. She stared at her weapon as if it had done the shooting independent of her.

Faye was quick to step in and take the gun from Lala, clearly afraid that the pretty Chinese woman would do something foolish—like express her remorse by handing the gun to Fargo.

"I'm sorry, Skye," Lala said, barely whispering.

"I almost believe you."

"Don't hate me, Skye."

"I'll try not to, Lala. But it won't be easy. I tend to dislike people who shoot me. I know it's petty of me but it's just the way I am."

He didn't want to give either of them the satisfaction of seeing how much pain he was in. He bunched his jaw muscles and tried to pretend that he didn't feel the raw stabbing agony shooting up his leg, or the hot blood flowing down his shin bone. Any man who could whomp on several grizzlies at a time could sure hold up to a minor problem like a deep leg wound.

"Well, Fargo, I guess we know where you stand with Lala now. We may as well get on with killing you."

"No last meal?"

"Afraid not."

"Can I see a priest?"

"Are you Roman Catholic?"

"No, but I'll convert."

She couldn't help herself. The beautiful Faye Manning smiled. "Face the lime pit, Fargo."

He reached out for a playful remark but none came. The lime pit. What a way to go, as people liked to say. Well, at least he'd be dead when the lime was stripping him to bone and then to damp ash. He'd come close to dying many times. It was the kind of life he led. But he'd never come close to dying like this. There was something undignified about being eaten alive in a lime pit. Better to have your last hurrah facing off against an angry bear or a tribe of hostiles. At least getting killed by grizzlies fit into the stories people told about him.

"I'm sorry, Skye." Lala again.

"Will you shut the hell up, Lala?" Faye Manning snapped. "The apologizing is getting very tiresome."

It was getting tiresome even to Fargo. She shoots you in the leg, she stands idly by while you die—and she's sorry?

"I said to face the pit, Fargo."

To make her point, she fired a bullet about one inch from the right side of his head. He couldn't help himself. It would have been more mythic to just stand there and not flinch. But he not only flinched, he moved over half a foot.

"The next one goes into your forehead, Fargo if you don't turn around."

"What's the difference? You're going to shoot me anyway."

"True. But I'm at least humane enough to shoot you in the back of the head. That way you won't know when it's coming."

"You should've been a nun, Faye, with a gentle soul like yours."

Before he glanced in Lala's direction, he hoped what he'd see was a pretty little Chinese gal getting ready to jump Faye Manning from behind and push her into the lime pit intended for Fargo. But that wasn't the way things had worked out. Lala stood to the left of Faye, simply watching as events unfolded.

I'm real real *real* sorry, Fargo, he could hear her saying to herself.

Uh-huh.

He would never be quite sure exactly what was said next. Something about "Pitch that gun to the floor."

The words were a soothing balm that charged him into action. Simultaneously he crouched to duck any bullets that might be coming his way, and swiveled around to see who had saved him.

Sandra Evans stood there with a rifle.

How the hell had she found him?

But there wasn't time for that now.

"Sandra!" he shouted as he saw Faye Manning lean to the side to draw a bead.

She'd kill the young woman for sure. Sandra looked so nervous, Fargo could see the barrel of her rifle bobbing up and down. She'd be easy pickings for Faye. She seemed almost transfixed by everything in front of her, as if she couldn't quite make up her mind what to look at.

Faye fired twice, hitting Sandra at least once. Sandra screamed.

Fargo dove for Faye's back, an explosion of pain in his leg as he grabbed her at the waist and whirled her around as if they were sharing some mad kind of dance.

But most dances didn't end with the lady involved falling face down into a lime pit, splattering lime in all directions.

Fargo heard noise behind him and saw that Sandra Evans, the right front shoulder of her white blouse muddied with blood, grabbing the ever-sorry Lala in a headlock with her left arm. Lala held a knife, but not for long. Sandra redoubled her headlock and then ran straight for the wall. The impact was such that the knife clattered to the floor instantly, and Lala, unconscious, collapsed next to it.

Fargo turned to the lime pit. By this time, Faye Manning was thoroughly covered with lime. Her color and texture were those of a crude piece of gray statuary. She was trying to sit up and crawl her way to freedom.

She alternated screaming, crying, and using some very unladylike words. Fargo did the only thing he could, given the circumstances. He took the shotgun from Sandra and took careful aim. Faye's screams approached inhuman levels and Fargo knew he had no choice. She had set him up and was prepared to kill him herself before Sandra had saved him, but to let another suffer like this, a woman especially, just wasn't his way. The rifle was an extension of his arm, the action was one of mercy. The Trailsman fired the weapon, taking off the top half of Faye's head. The kill was clean, her misery was over.

18

Fargo and Sandra both spent most of the night in town at the doc's office. In a small room in the back, Doc dealt with Sandra first, being a gentleman, as Lala lay in the other room, as one of McGinley's men stood watch, prepared to take her in as soon as she regained consciousness. Doc extracted the bullet from Sandra, cleansed the wound, and told her to sleep. He didn't have to talk long. She was snoring damply in moments. Even her snoring was cute.

When the doc started in on Fargo, he said, "She's mighty fine looking."

"She sure is."

"A fella could do a lot worse than marryin' her."

"Afraid I'm not the marryin' kind, Doc."

"Then what kind you be?"

"Oh, I like to ride around and have people shoot at me and call me names and spit on me and every once in a while try and hang me to break the monotony."

"Sounds like you have a lot of fun."

"Oh, I do. Especially when they try to hang me."

"You're the Trailsman, huh?"

"That's what they tell me," Fargo said. And then waited for the inevitable question that seemed to bedazzle folks in this part of the country.

"You really hold off a dozen grizzlies at the same time?" Doc said.

"I don't like to brag," Fargo said, "but it was eighteen. And a couple of them had guns."

"Guns?" the doc said, surprised. "I didn't know grizzlies came armed."

"They do," Fargo said, "when they come after the Trailsman."

LOOKING FORWARD!
The following is the opening
section of the next novel in the exciting
Trailsman series from Signet:

THE TRAILSMAN #268
New Mexico Nymph

New Mexico Territory, 1858—
The siren's song targets the strongest of men,
making the most beautiful of women
deadlier than a loaded six-shooter.

"Easy, boy, easy," Skye Fargo whispered to the Ovaro
as he carefully rode down the steep trail behind Early
Truffle's hideout.

Early and his boys had held up the stage that was
going from Lone Pine to Quake, New Mexico, a week
before, and Skye had been hired to go out and bring
them in, along with their captive.

Well, not exactly hired. Pressed into it was more to
the point.

Either way, here he was, in the New Mexico hills,
tippy-toeing down a sharp, wooded slope, trying to
sneak up on the gang.

It was early morning, barely dawn. Smoke rose in

a thin plume from the cabin's chimney, likely smoke left over from last night's dying fire. Early, despite his name, didn't rise with the sun.

These boys had not only held up the stage, but they'd killed the driver and kidnapped young Mrs. Diego Madrid, the bride of Señor Diego Francisco Esteban Rodriguez Madrid, owner of the second-largest rancho in New Mexico, and a friend of Fargo's from way back.

Sort of. Fargo hadn't reminded Madrid that the last time they'd met, Madrid had lost fifty-seven dollars to Fargo and hadn't paid it. Of course, a little range war had broken out right in the middle of the card game, but Fargo really didn't think that was any excuse.

If Fargo came back with his wife—and the Los Galgos payroll that the stage had been carrying— Madrid might be a little more keen on remembering that small pot.

Or so Fargo hoped.

The Ovaro, a tall, gleaming, black and white stallion, made it down the slope without making a sound, and Fargo reined him to a halt while he was still back in the woods. Or at least, the low, spotty vegetation that passed for woods in these parts. He looped the horse's reins over a branch, then crept forward.

Scuttling to the cabin's side, he moved forward, along the outside wall, until he was just under the window. He took a careful peek inside.

It was just as he thought.

Early Truffle was asleep in his bunk. Two other men—Roy Spriggs and Two-Bit Thompson, Fargo thought—dozed in bedrolls on the floor. The only person awake was the extremely attractive Mrs. Madrid, whose brown, Spanish eyes grew round as saucers when she turned her head and spied him.

Fargo held a finger to his lips, then ducked back down.

She'd be no help to him. She was bound and

gagged, seated on a hard chair in the center of the room. He didn't want to wake the outlaws and put them on the alert, even though there was a chance one of them might come outside and make for easier pickings.

But Mrs. Madrid might get hurt in the process. Fargo didn't want that.

And so he silently made his way around the crude cabin, to the door. Carefully, he tried the latch.

It was ajar, and the door softly creaked open at his touch.

He couldn't believe his luck.

But when he took one step inside, the floorboards gave him away. He froze at the painful creak. Early turned over, but didn't wake up. Fargo wasn't so lucky with Two-Bit.

Two-Bit's eyes popped open, and half a second later he pulled his gun.

Fargo fired before he did, though.

Fargo fired again at Roy Spriggs, who was by that time scrambling free of his blankets, gun in hand.

Mrs. Madrid screamed, despite the gag in her mouth, as Fargo wheeled back to face Early Truffle. But Early's timing was off. He was just reaching for his holstered gun, hung on a peg on the wall, when Fargo cocked his gun again and said, "Not so fast, Early."

"Damn you, Trailsman!" Early snapped, although his voice was still a little groggy with sleep. "Where'd you come from, anyhow? How'd you get in on this deal?"

"Never you mind," Fargo said. "Now, suppose you busy yourself getting Mrs. Madrid untied." When Early, grumbling, moved to untie her, Fargo added, "There's a good feller, Early."

Free at last, Mrs. Madrid rushed into his arms, nearly knocking the gun from his hands. He managed to catch her and still keep it aimed at Early, though.

"Oh, thank you, thank you, sir!" she babbled. She turned out to be a staggering beauty underneath that gag, too. He had to keep on reminding himself that she was a missus, not a Miss, and that her husband was a friend of his. Sort of.

"The name's Fargo, ma'am," he said when she stopped for air. "Skye Fargo. Your husband sent me."

"Bless him! Bless you! Kill this last animal!"

She made a grab for his gun hand, as if she could force him to pull the trigger, but Fargo held her off.

"Hold on, lady," he said. "Your husband wants 'em in one piece." He looked over at the floor, where Two-Bit Thompson lay dead. Roy Spriggs wasn't doing much better. "Well, one'a them, at least," he added. He jerked the gun's barrel at Early. "Get your hands out in front of you, Early."

Mrs. Madrid set a fist on either hip. "Who is in charge, now, Mister Stage Robber?"

Early made a face.

Fargo handed Mrs. Madrid his spare pistol, telling her to aim it at Early and shoot if need be, and he then got busy with the rope.

"You say that perhaps we will reach town tomorrow?" Mrs. Madrid asked.

They had camped for the night. Early Truffle was hogtied over by the horses, and Fargo was just dishing up some grub.

"Yes," he said. "Tomorrow."

It wasn't soon enough if you asked him. Mrs. Madrid was a beauty, all right. Her looks, in fact, were nearly transcendental. Dark, Spanish eyes, long lashes, the face of an angel, and the body to match.

But she had turned out to be a bitch of the first water. That afternoon, when Fargo had asked for her first name, she had snidely said, "You may call me Mrs. Madrid. Or Señora Madrid, if you are so inclined."

She'd said it in a way that made him feel like she was addressing a servant, not her savior.

It kind of pissed him off, to be truthful. He didn't remark on it, though. He just figured that he'd soon be shed of her, and he'd never have to see her again. So in the meantime, he only spoke when spoken to.

It was easier.

Except that as she took her plate, she asked, "They have found my sister?"

Hell, he hadn't even known she had one. And if her sister was lost, why had she waited so long to ask, anyhow?

"You lose her?" Fargo asked, settling back with his supper. "Careless of you."

She didn't understand the dig. She just looked at him oddly, then said, "She lost herself. To the West. You do not know of this?"

Fargo bit a corner off a biscuit. Chewing, he shook his head.

"Well . . . ," Mrs. Madrid said, and gave him a look that finished her sentence. The look said, *If you are not important enough to know, then perhaps I shouldn't have spoken.*

Fargo didn't press her on it. He was too hungry, and too annoyed with her already. He didn't need to be told once more that he was no better than a piece of shit under her shoe.

Especially by the stuck-up wife of a man who owed him fifty-seven dollars.

They pulled into Quake early the next afternoon. Fargo turned Early Truffle—and the payroll—over to the town sheriff, drew him a map of where he could find the hastily dug graves of Roy Spriggs, who had died, and of Two-Bit Thompson, who had died as well.

The sheriff thanked him politely, then locked up the money and threw the map away.

He also gave Fargo a voucher for three hundred dollars, which surprised Fargo to no end. "This for Early?" he asked. "Didn't think there could be more than fifty bucks on his head."

"Oh, he knocked over a tradin' post outside Santa Fe," the sheriff replied. "Shot the owner. These things add up, you know."

Fargo stuck the voucher in his pocket. "I guess they do," he said with a shrug.

And then he escorted Mrs. Diego Madrid up to the hotel, and her husband.

When he knocked at the door of the Madrids' suite, Madrid didn't answer it himself. Rather, a butler, classically English, did.

"Madam," he said, showing no emotion whatsoever. He bowed just slightly. "Welcome home. I trust you are unharmed."

She didn't answer him, just walked on past. Fargo just stood there watching her go, and then realized the butler was still standing there, waiting.

"Testy, ain't she?" he asked.

"One would believe so, sir," said the butler. "Mr. Madrid would like to see you as well, at your convenience."

Fargo stepped through the door and took off his hat. "He'd better. The bastard owes me fifty-seven bucks from two years ago."

The butler, leading the way down the hall, said, "I'm terribly sorry, sir."

"Don't call me sir."

"Yes, sir."

Fargo gave up. He was also just beginning to realize that Madrid had the whole top floor of this building, not just a suite of rooms. He was impressed. The cow-ranching business must be profitable these days.

Just then, the butler stopped before a door and rapped softly.

"Enter!" shouted a voice—Madrid's.

Fargo expected to find him with his wife, but he was alone when the butler opened the door.

"You've found her?" Madrid asked, brightening when he saw that it was Fargo.

"She's around here somewhere," Fargo offered.

"Indeed, sir," said the butler. "Shall I—"

Madrid waved him into silence. "No, no, Foster. She will come when she is ready. She is bathing the trail dust away, no?" he asked Fargo, but didn't wait for a reply. He simply gestured the butler out, then gestured Fargo to one of two leather chairs beside the window.

"My friend," Madrid said, joining him in the opposite chair. He reached for the brandy. He said, "I am so pleased!" He paused. "She was unharmed?"

Fargo nodded. "None the worse for wear. And I'm happy for you, Madrid," Fargo said, leaning back. It was a nice chair. "Be happier if you'd pay up on that gambling debt."

Madrid actually looked surprised. "I owe you money, Fargo? From when?"

"From a few years back," Fargo said. He took the small glass that Madrid offered and swirled the amber-colored liquid. "You remember when we were in that seven-card-stud game, and young Danny Florez came runnin' in smack in the middle of it and—"

Madrid smacked his forehead. "Ay! How careless! Fargo, please forgive me. I had forgotten completely. Here, let me make it right."

Madrid rose and crossed the room to his desk, and pulled out a black velvet pouch, then a fistful of coins. He returned to Fargo, who was still holding his untouched brandy, and he began counting out coins from those in his hand. "It was fifty-eight, was it not?"

"Fifty-seven."

"Honest to the last penny!" Madrid said with a grin. "A man can always count on you, Fargo. There," he said, placing the final coin in Fargo's hand. "Fifty-seven. And your reward for the return of my lovely

Rosa." He plunked the velvet bag into Fargo's hand, too. "I cannot tell you what a happy man you make me."

Fargo sat there, staring at it. "You mean, there was a reward?" He meant that several ways.

"Yes, certainly!" Madrid sat down again, and he looked suddenly thunderstruck. "You mean to tell me that you have gone out on the trail of my wife and these miscreants with no thought of a reward? That you did it out of friendship and friendship alone?"

Actually, Fargo had done it just to get that fifty-seven dollars back, but he suspected now wasn't the time to mention it.

He shrugged.

"How did I come to deserve such a friend?" Diego asked the ceiling, and ostensibly, someone far above it. He gripped Fargo's arm, slopping Fargo's brandy just a little.

"Don't go gettin' all choked up, Madrid," Fargo said, gently freeing his arm. Madrid always had been on the emotional side. It was that hot-blooded Spanish flair, Fargo guessed. He pocketed the coins and the little pouch, though, just in case Madrid changed his mind about the reward.

"You will stay to dine with us?" Madrid asked, and Fargo didn't have the heart to turn him down. "Yes," Madrid continued. "You will stay. And I think I will have another job for such a good friend. One I would only trust to you."

Fargo lifted his brandy and toasted Madrid, and then drank. If it would pay well—and right about now, Fargo was pretty damned sure that it would—he was all for it.

No other series has this much historical action!

THE TRAILSMAN

Available wherever books are sold, or
to order call: 1-800-788-6262

SIGNET HISTORICAL FICTION (0451)

Ralph
Cotton

JUSTICE 19496-9

A powerful land baron uses his political influence to persuade local law-men to release his son from a simple assault charge. The young man, however, is actually the leader of the notorious Half Moon Gang—a mad pack of killers with nothing to lose!

BLOOD MONEY 20676-2

Bounty hunters have millions of reasons to catch J.T. Priest—but Marshal Hart needs only one. And he's sworn to bring the killer down...mano-a-mano.

DEVIL'S DUE 20394-1

The second book in Cotton's "Dead or Alive" series. The *Pistoleros* gang were the most vicious outlaws around—but Hart and Roth thought they had them under control....Until the jailbreak.

JURISDICTION 20547-2

Young Arizona Ranger Sam Burrack has vowed to bring down a posse of murderous outlaws—and save the impressionable young boy they've befriended.

VENGEANCE IS A BULLET 20799-8

Arizona Ranger Sam Burrack must hunt down a lethal killer whose mind is bent by revenge and won't stop killing until the desert is piled high with the bodies of those who wronged him.

Available wherever books are sold, or
to order call: 1-800-788-6262

SIGNET

Charles G. West
HERO'S STAND

Up in the Montana mountains, Canyon Creek is the perfect little town for Simon Fry and his men to hole up for the winter. The folks are friendly enough to open their homes to eight perfect strangers—and gullible enough to believe that Fry's gang is a militia sent to protect them from hostile Indians.

Jim Culver is new in town, but he knows something isn't right about Simon Fry's "militia." They seem more interested in intimidating people than helping them. Anyone who questions them ends up dead or driven out. Someone has to step forward to protect the people of Canyon Creek from their new "protectors."

That someone is Jim Culver. And this sleepy town is about to wake up with a bang.

0-451-20822-6

Available wherever books are sold, or
to order call: 1-800-788-6262

S805